R.H. Hull (Ray Hull) was born and raised on their family farms located in the same area of Kansas as the Old Order Mennonite families about whom this novel is written. He received his early education in the same two-room rural school that the Mennonite children mentioned in this story also attended. He lived in this area of Kansas with his parents from childhood into young adulthood, working with his father on their farms. Throughout his young adulthood, he maintained his relationships with his Mennonite friends and colleagues.

Currently, after completing his doctorate in neuroscience, he is a successful published author of thirty-two books including four books co-authored with New York Times bestselling author, Jim Stovall, twenty-two well-recognized textbooks on communication disorders and communicating in professional life, a successful novel entitled *A Place Called Eden,* and most recently, *The Art of De-Stressing: Removing the Most Stressful Obstacles to Personal and Professional Success.* He is also a columnist, and a nationally known presenter at over 600 conferences and conventions on *The Art of Communication in Professional Life* across the U.S. and other countries.

To my lovely wife and my beautiful daughter.

R.H. Hull

Cloud County: A Love Story

AUSTIN MACAULEY PUBLISHERS™

LONDON • CAMBRIDGE • NEW YORK • SHARJAH

Ordering Information
Quantity sales: Special discounts are available on quantity purchases by corporations, associations, and others. For details, contact the publisher at the address below.

Publisher's Cataloging-in-Publication data
Hull, R.H.
Cloud County: A Love Story

ISBN 9798891551404 (Paperback)
ISBN 9798891551411 (ePub e-book)

Library of Congress Control Number: 2023923061

www.austinmacauley.com/us

First Published 2024
Austin Macauley Publishers LLC
40 Wall Street, 33rd Floor, Suite 3302
New York, NY 10005
USA

mail-usa@austinmacauley.com
+1 (646) 5125767

I am indebted to my friends and colleagues of various Mennonite Orders whom I have known for many years. The premise of this story comes from what I learned from them during our friendships that have lasted from our grade school years on into young adulthood. Our lengthy conversations over the years have given me insights into a wonderful culture of gentle and caring people.

Chapter 1

When Adam Yoder's family moved from their farm in Pennsylvania onto their new farm in Kansas, Adam was enrolled in the eighth grade at Fairmont Rural School. Fairmont Rural School was in a rather remote, primarily Old Order Mennonite farming community in Cloud County, Kansas. The school had two classrooms, one was designated for the lower grades and one was designated for the upper grades. The lower grades were first grade first through fourth. And the upper grades were fifth grade through eighth.

There were three students in the eighth grade, including two girls and Adam. When he first caught a glimpse of Sarah Goering, who was assigned to the seat directly in front of him, he immediately felt his pulse jump. She was, he felt, one of the prettiest girls he had ever seen! And when she turned in her seat and introduced herself to him, he knew that he must have developed a rosy glow about his face, and he felt his heart beating loudly. As he started to reply, he was embarrassed as he stammered through his name. But he was relieved when she told him that she was happy that he had joined their eighth-grade class.

As he got to know Sarah better, he realized that she was, as far as he was concerned, both the smartest and most beautiful girl at Fairmont Rural School. Besides that, she was also the best softball player on the upper grade team. Since the Fairmont Rural School was a small two-room rural school, the school had two softball teams—one for the upper grade classroom and one for the lower grade classroom. The lower grade allowed all students to play in rotation, so everyone had an opportunity to participate. On the 'upper grade' softball team, there were six players who were selected according to their ability to play in various positions. Sarah was selected as their best and bravest catcher. Adam was elected to be their pitcher.

Sarah, being one of the more mature students, was able to catch and throw the ball more efficiently than the smaller children. Aside from her athletic prowess, Adam Yoder saw that at 14 years, she was blossoming into a lovely young woman. At least, that is what he had noticed.

It disturbed Sarah that when playing softball, she had to maintain a catcher's squat position behind the batter's box. It angered her that besides the very unladylike stance she was required to maintain, she still had to wear her long, rather heavy conservative dress of the Old Order Mennonites, a very inconvenient mode of dress for a softball player, particularly because she was the catcher. Since the length of the dresses reached almost to her ankles, she couldn't move with the speed that she needed for that position on the team.

Further, she had a difficult time attempting to convince her parents that she did not want to wear a dress while playing softball. And besides, the traditional white cap with the long shoulder-length straps that she was required to wear didn't fit under the catcher's mask.

So, in order to maintain the air of propriety required of girls of the Old Order Mennonite doctrine, she was required to pull her dress snugly over her knees and down around her ankles while she was behind the batter's box. However, that didn't allow her much maneuverability, particularly when the batter happened to hit a foul ball.

But, despite those inconveniences, she was still required by her parents to wear both the long dress and the traditional Old Order Mennonite cap. She desperately wanted to wear blue jeans like other girls she had seen while she and her mother shopped at the grocery store in the nearby town of Wheatland, Kansas, and those who she saw when her school played softball against other rural schools in their county whose students were 'of the world'; in other words, not of their conservative Mennonite Order.

But all the girls who attended Fairmont Rural School wore the same long plain dresses that were designed to be no higher than 10 inches above the ankle, dark brown hose with plain brown shoes along with white caps that were usually perched toward the back of their head. The caps had long straps that usually hung loosely about their shoulders. Since they all attended the same Wheatland Mennonite Church, they all dressed similarly.

The church they attended each Sunday and each Wednesday evening for Prayer Meeting with their parents sat majestically in an open field. It had the appearance of a huge white three-story wooden ship that had become stranded out in a flat field of wheat in the middle of Cloud County, Kansas.

Chapter 2

From the first day of attendance at Fairmont Rural School, Adam Yoder had admired Sarah Goering. His admiration of her lasted throughout their years of attendance and he felt strongly that he was in love with her, at least he thought it was love. Even though at age 15 years, he was thought by his parents to be too young to know what love consisted of, he felt that the strong feelings that he had for Sarah simply had to those of love, or at least close to it. Both he and Sarah were in the final year of their schooling at Fairmont Rural School.

The reason for that year being the final year of their schooling was because, according to their Old Order Mennonite tradition, at the conclusion of the eighth grade when young people were at about 14 to 15 years of age, they were of an age to begin to take their place in their community.

Their Mennonite Order felt that young women were to begin taking their place in the home learning to care for a home, cook, and learn the economic duties of budgeting for the many aspects of home management. Those included, among others, the caring of children and other such duties that involved 'home economics' that they did not learn about at school. Some other areas that young women learned about involved a life that would in all probability be located on a farm including the care and feeding of farm animals, milking cows by hand, butchering chickens for frying or baking, curing ham and bacon, and many other such tasks. Those were important for women of their Mennonite Order and heritage to learn in anticipation of marriage and a family that would in all probability soon be a major part of their young life.

Young men were also expected to conclude their formal education at the end of the eighth grade. At the conclusion of the eighth grade, they continued their education by learning farming techniques from their fathers and grandfathers. Those included the care and feeding of dairy and/or beef cattle, correct methods of tilling and caring for the soil, the planting of crops, the art of butchering and cutting meat, and others in anticipation of assuming duties on the family farm when their father could no longer actively continue working. At that point, the farm, in accordance with their Old Order Mennonite heritage, would usually be turned over to the son.

At some point after graduating from the eighth grade, and usually at around age 17 or 18 years, some young men entered two years of what was called 'Voluntary Service' that has been a part of numerous Mennonite denominations in the United States for many years. Voluntary Service is a national and international service in lieu of entering the military. When they reached age 18 years, Mennonite young men of their Alderman Order generally registered with their local Draft Board as Pacifists.

Voluntary Service gave those young men the opportunity to serve within the U.S. or other countries, wherever they were sent to reconstruct houses that had been destroyed by storms or war, reconstruct villages in underdeveloped countries that may have been destroyed by war or weather, and many other opportunities to serve in lieu of entering the military. During Voluntary Service, they would also frequently learn a trade as carpenters, plumbers, electricians, or others that could later serve those young men well if they chose to enter one of them after being dismissed from their Voluntary Service obligations. Those trades could also support their farming income as an add-on vocation when farming duties slowed during the winter months.

When children of those conservative Mennonite families married, usually at a young age of 18 or 19 years, the groom's father and mother, and perhaps with support from the bride's parents, would build the couple a house that would sometimes be located on the groom's family's farm. There, the groom would farm with his father, preparing to assume those duties at some time in the future, and the young bride and groom would begin their own family. Thus, the continuum of family that would move on into the next generation.

Marriages were sometimes 'gently' arranged. That is, the parents of a likely couple would suggest, sometimes rather strongly that a young man and young woman from their respective families 'might' consider getting together for purposes of dating, hoping that the relationship would blossom into the couple becoming 'paired'. Being 'paired' referred to an early exclusive commitment that could frequently grow into an engagement, and then marriage.

In that Mennonite community, marriage was not to take place unless it united a young man and young woman of their same Mennonite heritage and Order. The problem there was that there were few potential females and males as potential mates who were not somehow related, that is members of the same family. Most were at least first or second cousins, and some parents and grandparents were not aware of the potential genetic dangers of intermarriage between relatives. On the other hand, most of their children were aware since they had learned about the potential negative effects of intermarriage in the 'Health' course that they took during their 8th grade in school. Their goal was generally not to marry a cousin, no matter what their parents suggested.

Adam Yoder felt that he was blessed since he was of no familial relation to anyone in Cloud County. His family had moved to Kansas after his father sold their large farms in Pennsylvania in anticipation of buying an equal or greater amount of land in central Kansas. So genetically, Adam was absolutely no relation to Sarah. Therefore, he would be among the few males in that community and the Wheatland Mennonite Church who was not even a distant relative of anyone who lived there. He somehow wanted Sarah to know that but was unsure how to bring the subject up with her.

Chapter 3

The reason Abraham Yoder, Adam's father, had investigated buying land in central Kansas was that people who were considered to be 'of the world' were moving into the farming community where the Yoders had lived in Farmland County, Pennsylvania. They were buying small parcels of land with the intent of becoming 'gentleman' farmers, but still working their jobs in the nearby city. They were moving into what used to be the Yoder's quiet Mennonite and Amish community. That was of some concern to those who had for many years established their farms there and had maintained their simple life away from 'the world' as they called it. Many of the Mennonite farmers were selling their land to those 'of the world' and moving to other communities.

After reading about farmland in central Kansas and discovering that the soil was black and rich and without the rocks, the tree sprouts and roots that Adam's father had to contend with on their land in Pennsylvania, a move to that part of the country was attractive. Further, he also discovered that the area of Kansas he was interested in had a fairly large community of conservative Old Order Mennonites that was very similar to his family's religious Order. Therefore, he thought that it would not only be perfect for farming, but also a comfortable location for his family since they would be in a community where there was a large and active Old Order Mennonite church. He also found that the price of land in Pennsylvania was much higher than in central Kansas. Therefore, rather than the 640 acres that he currently farmed, he might be able to buy two sections of land, a whopping 1280 acres! He would suddenly, therefore, be the owner of a very large farm in Kansas as compared to the one he owned in Pennsylvania.

He researched the available land in central Kansas and was soon able to locate the acreage he desired in Cloud County, the same county as the Wheatland Mennonite Church. He was pleased that he was able to locate two sections of land that were in a single large piece, rather than in several different smaller acreages that he currently owned in Pennsylvania that required moving equipment from one place to the other during harvest, plowing and other aspects of summer farm work.

He found that Cloud County is made up of several small rural towns, great rolling fields of wheat that were owned primarily by Old Order Mennonite farmers who had moved there because of the fertile soil and abundant water from the annual rain fall, and subterranean water from a huge underground reservoir called the Kansan Aquafer.

So, after a number of family conferences and determining the benefit of buying land in central Kansas, they sold their farm in Pennsylvania, and finalized the sale on the Kansas acreage. Adam's father was suddenly considered to be a large and potentially prosperous land owner in an equally conservative Mennonite community to that where he and his family had lived in Pennsylvania.

As the number of Old Order Mennonite families settled in Cloud County, some of the families who were non-Mennonite and 'of the world', in other words members of other churches that were located in Wheatland, Kansas, the closest town of any size in that part of the state, thought that perhaps the conservative Mennonites were Amish. But, the Yoder family was not of the Amish, but rather a member of the Old Older branch of the Aldeman Mennonites, nearly the same as those in the community where they were moving in central Kansas.

They were conservative in dress and conservative in their social order, and in that way were similar to those who are of the Amish community. However, rather than horses and buggies, they, drove plain cars that had no hub caps, or chrome, and were a plain color of black, brown, dark blue, or gray. Cars were considered a more desirable mode of transportation compared to the horse and buggies that their ancestors had used. They also used modern farm equipment rather than the horse-drawn equipment used by those of the nearby Amish community, that was the only other convenience that one would consider 'of the world'. However, rather than 'of the world', that type of farm equipment was considered absolutely essential if they wanted to work their farms efficiently and in an economically sensible manner. And, they were very sensible people, both economically, socially, and personally.

The women wore the typical conservatively designed long dresses that were generally eight-ten inches above the ankle. Their hair was usually braided and worn as 'pig tails' by female children, and wound tightly about the head of women. The young women wore white caps with long slender straps that, if they felt less conservative on a given day, hung loosely about their shoulders. Otherwise, the straps were tied beneath their chin. Mature women wore black or dark blue caps or bonnets, and usually tied the strap under their chin. They wore dark hose and rather non-stylish plain shoes.

Men generally wore beards that were usually carefully trimmed, with no mustache since a mustache was considered 'of the world', homemade jeans or overalls or slacks, and homemade shirts with no collar. Their clothes were made primarily by the women of their household.

The phrase 'of the world' referred to those from outside of their Aldeman Mennonite Order and community. They were those who lived in non-Mennonite communities or cities that were not like theirs both in their social and religious lives. In 'the world', girls and women wore store-bought dresses, blue jeans, shorts and tee shirts in the summer, colorful lipstick, rouge, stylish hair styles and other signs of 'the world'. They did not wear the traditional cap of the Mennonite women, or dresses that were made of plain cotton cloth with puffed sleeves, dark hose and plain shoes.

Those of 'the world' drove cars that had chrome decorations, shiny hub caps and were painted many different colors. Men wore store-bought shirts and slacks, blue jeans and fancy shoes. They were not pacifists, and some became military soldiers who went off to war rather than the Voluntary Service that Mennonite young men engaged in.

That was what was meant by 'of the world'; those who were not of their Order or heritage of resisting the ways 'of the world'; a life without the 'frills' of the world, without television or radios, or electricity in some homes, some even without cars or trucks or tractors for their farms, and without store-bought clothes or fancy shoes, or collars on shirts. And if they owned a car, it had to be very plain with colors of black, brown, gray or navy blue. Further, the cars had to be without hubcaps or chrome or other decorations, all of which were considered 'of the world'.

Chapter 4

At the conclusion of the eighth grade, their final year of formal schooling for the Old Order Mennonite children, both the boys and girls were celebrated with a formal graduation ceremony where the boys wore their finest hand-sewn suites made by their mother, and the girls wore their finest hand-sewn dresses that were usually sewn by them with extra care, and with the prettiest cloth that they could find. Rather than relatively plain cotton material that they usually used to sew everyday dresses, they, accompanied by their mother, were sometimes allowed to go to a fabric store in Wheatland, Kansas, to pick out the material from which they would sew their graduation dress. That was a happy occasion since it would be the first time they could make their own decision regarding the color and design of the cloth from which they would sew their dress. And rather than plain cotton material, they could choose fabric with flowers or other pretty colors.

That time was quickly drawing near for the students of the Cloud County, Kansas rural schools. The school year was coming to a close and Adam was beginning to feel a sense of foreboding—of emptiness. He didn't know if Sarah cared at all for him. His feelings for her had been secretly kept within his heart for such a long time. He felt that his feelings for her were of love. He had been taught by his parents, and by attending the Wheatland Mennonite Church that lust was a sin. But Adam felt that the feelings that he had for Sarah were not those of lust. He genuinely felt that his feelings for Sarah were those of love, so he wasn't committing a sin. He wasn't sure if they were actual feelings of love since he wasn't exactly sure what 'love' meant. He knew, however, that he cared for her more than he had ever cared for anyone in his young life.

Even though he and Sarah were in the 8th grade together, and there was only one other student in that grade at school, he had no idea if Sarah even knew he existed except when he was the pitcher for their Fairmont School softball team, and she was his catcher. He admired her. He thought that she was wonderful. She was smart, kind, beautiful, and very brave to place herself so close to a batter who was swinging at a pitched ball that she was supposed to catch if the batter missed it!

Adam wondered, *How do I convince Sarah that I care for her? How do I tell her? What words could I use that would not cause her to reject me?* He had to do something quickly since their final year of schooling was quickly coming to a close. Adam felt a sense of urgency to do something dramatically that would let Sarah know how he felt about her. And, whatever he said had to be so powerful that as they grew older and could begin dating, she would remember how he felt when they were at the conclusion of the 8th grade.

But how could that be done? Adam felt at a loss since Sarah, although she was the best athlete in their school she was also rather aloof. She remained rather distant and difficult to get to know.

Chapter 5

Then, something happened that Adam would not have imagined would occur. One day toward the conclusion of their final semester, a new boy came to their school and joined them in the eighth grade. He was obviously not Mennonite. He seemed to be what the Old Order Aldeman Mennonite Church called 'of the world'.

The new boy's name was Richie Johnson. He would be the only boy in Fairmont School who was not of the Aldeman Mennonite Order—he was of Lutheran heritage. And the Mennonite girls of his school apparently thought that Richie was good-looking and worldly. He wore 'worldly' clothes, fancy shoes that he called loafers rather than the plain heavy 'farm' shoes that the other boys had to wear. Further, he obviously had his hair cut at a barber shop rather than by his mother as Adam had to, and his father drove him to school in shiny car that had chrome on the sides and shiny hubcaps.

Adam felt a twinge of envy when he observed the girls talking to Richie, giggling, smiling at him, obviously trying to catch his attention. Those girls were not supposed to be associating with him since he was 'of the world', but they were, even though they were not supposed to!

Now, Adam had to move with even greater speed. His sense of urgency was greater now. But, to do what? What could he do to convince Sarah that he was as exciting as Richie? Time was running short since graduation was arriving quickly! When Adam told his parents about the new boy who had moved to Fairmount School, they seemed to already know about his family. They had moved to Richie's grandfather's farm that was located in the Lutheran community that was about ten miles north of Fairmont School.

So, Adam thought that his only salvation was that Richie came from a family 'of the world' who attended the New Horizon Lutheran Church that was quite a distance from their Aldeman Mennonite community. So at least he was not a member of their community, and hopefully would be gone and never heard of again at the end of the school year and after graduation.

As the days wore on, and Richie had settled in at their school, his newness was beginning to wear off. In fact, he appeared so self-assured and aloof that the girls actually began to avoid him as much as was possible within the small space of that tiny two-room school building. He seemed to have taken on an air of superiority. His store-bought clothes began to lose something that had attracted the girls earlier. He possessed an air of 'class' that didn't belong in their school or community, and students began to sense it. The boys of the Old Order Aldeman Mennonite community had to have their hair trimmed and cut by their mothers at home. Plus, their clothes were usually homemade by the women of their households. Their shoes and hats were purchased at the Eden General Store, in Eden, Kansas. Their shoes were rather roughhewn and heavy, and the hats that the boys were supposed to wear were made out of heavy felt and either dark brown or black, with a flat round brim.

But, as the newness and worldliness of Richie began to wane, and life at Fairmont School began to return to normal, Adam was still faced with the difficulty that he had been facing for some time. That was Sarah. He wanted her to know that he felt, in his own mind, that she was the loveliest, smartest, most talented girl he had ever met. To Adam, she was all those things.

But Richie also had his eye on Sarah. He apparently felt that in her own rather plain manner, she was pretty and desirable. However, she had stopped paying attention to him, and even in the small space of their two-room school, she was avoiding him as much as possible. She wasn't actually trying to avoid him; it was that she had apparently lost interest. He was not of their kind, not of their Mennonite Order, so she knew in her own mind that there was no reason to pay any real attention to him—to acknowledge him in a positive way. At least she was trying to convince herself of that inevitable conclusion to any relationship with someone who was not of their Mennonite Order.

Chapter 6

Suddenly, the last day of school potluck dinner and student performances were upon them. Those were used historically each year as a celebration at the close of the school year. The student performances consisted of singing prepared by the students with their teacher as the Director. The chorus of the Upper Room consisting of the 5th, 6th, 7th, and 8th grades, and the chorus of the Lower Grades consisting of the 1st, 2nd, 3rd, and 4th grades were to each sing two songs. Also, a one-act play entitled, 'Johnny Appleseed' was being prepared. Adam's favorite teacher was the Director of the play. Since Adam had a very nice singing voice, he had been selected to play the lead role of Johnny Appleseed in the play. He had to transform from a young man into old age during the play and was to sing three songs.

The final scene was when a white-bearded elderly Johnny Appleseed walked slowly off into a grove of beautifully blooming apple trees, and on into Heaven. It was to be a very touching scene. Although he was to sing three solos, the major solo entitled 'The Lord Is Good to Me' was at a pitch that was beginning to be too high for him. And, although he was doing a fairly good job in rehearsal, what his teacher had feared was occurring. He was rapidly entering puberty, and his voice was changing and assuming a lower pitch. So, it cracked on occasion on the high notes of that song. But he was hoping with all his heart that he would do well enough to impress Sarah! That was his greatest concern.

Classes were held that morning, final grades were handed to each student by their teacher, Mrs. Thurman for the lower grade classroom, and Mrs. Hamilton for the upper grade classroom. Goodbyes by the two teachers were said, tears were shed, and students were to give the student across their isle a hug and to say 'goodbye' at least for the summer for those in the 5th, 6th, and 7th grades, and those in the 4th grade in the lower grade room who would be moving into the upper grade room in the fall to enter fifth grade.

A final goodbye was said by those in the 8th grade who would be going through their graduation in the Wheatland, Kansas Community Building the next day, and then on into their new lives. It was a very sad day for them since upon graduation from the eighth grade, they essentially became adults.

There was a sumptuous potluck dinner consisting of many of the traditional Prussian, German and Russian dishes of their heritages that included among others bratwurst, knockwurst, baked pork chops in gravy, oven baked German potato salad, sauerkraut and sausage, and others along with many tasty desserts, coffee for the adults, and homemade ice cream that was churned right there at the school building. Both the adults and the school children were full and satisfied after experiencing a wonderful meal of some of the traditional foods of their Mennonite Order and the heritage of the families who farmed in that community.

Almost immediately upon completing the meal and desert, and after finishing a good cup of coffee and a dish of homemade ice cream, the eating utensils were picked up and washed in the school kitchen by the women while the men sat, drank more coffee and talked of crops, farm prices and other matters of importance to farmers.

Adam could not eat much, nor could the others who were in the lower and upper grades. They were nervously getting ready for their choruses and the play that was the highlight of the afternoon last day of school celebration. Adam simply did not feel like eating. He had too much on his mind including his lines in the play, the songs he was to sing, and wondering what would happen if he mustered the courage to tell Sarah all that he intended to tell her.

Well—that moment came rather unexpectantly. The upper grade choir was ready to begin a final brief rehearsal before their performances that afternoon and to make sure that the play that Adam was staring in was ready for its single performance. The upper grade choir always stood away from the backstage in a small hallway before walking onto the stage. They would eventually walk onto the stage to stand on multi-level risers that some of the Mennonite men in the community had built for their school. The curtain that covered the front of the small stage was now pulled firmly shut so the family members in the school basement would not see them. Many of the adults were still eating dessert, and Mrs. Hamilton who doubled as their music teacher did not want those sitting at the lunch tables to see the students while they rehearsed some rough spots in one of the choir numbers just prior to their performance.

Chapter 7

Adam had planned a potential strategy that would allow him to say a few words to Sarah before the performances began. His strategy was that when everyone was standing back stage in the hallway ready to walk onto the risers on stage to rehearse, if Sarah happened for any reason to move away from the others, it would be a perfect time to talk to her and tell her of his feelings for her. But he would have to say what he intended to say quickly. There would only be a couple of minutes to say it all, so he would have to move quickly.

And then, a miracle happened. Sarah left the group! She walked quickly toward the water fountain in the outer hallway to get a drink of water before the performance. Adam swallowed hard, and quickly left the group to follow her. The problem was that several other girls apparently had the same idea and followed Sarah to the water fountain. But, as he approached her, she moved slightly away from the others in order to allow them to have their drink of water first. Seeing his opportunity, he quickly followed her to where she was now standing. He had no idea what he was going to say in such a brief period of time, but he knew he had to say something. It was time—it was actually beyond time to reveal his feelings for her.

As he approached Sarah, she had just moved away from the water fountain, and had moved from the other girls so they could satisfy their thirst. As she looked up after moving away from the water fountain, she saw Adam standing near her. Assuming that Adam was there to also get a drink of water, she moved further to the side, and waited momentarily. Adam looked at her, became embarrassed and he looked down at his feet. But, since Sarah was still standing near him, he cleared his throat and quickly began to talk.

He began, "Sarah, I've been trying to get the courage to tell you something for a long time now." He started to continue, but Sarah interrupted him to say that they needed to return to the chorus. But, Adam stopped her… "No!" Adam said with such force that it startled her. "I want to tell you something!" He hesitated only momentarily, and then with a rush of adrenaline, he moved forward and the words came pouring out. "I…I…I have wanted to tell you that for the past three years, I have had 'feelings' for you. I know I am too young to know what love is, but my feelings for you, I feel, are those of love."

Suddenly, they both seemed to lose track of time. The choir was beginning their final rehearsal without them, but it didn't seem to matter at that moment. Anna looked directly into Adam's eyes and replied, "Oh Adam, I want you to know that in all the months and years we have known each other here in Fairmont School, I have had similar feelings for you. I just did not know how to tell you."

Adam was suddenly at a loss for words. Sarah had secretly felt strongly that she cared for him—feelings that were similar to those Adam had for her. They had wasted so much time! But what would they have done differently? They had been together in the two-room confines of Fairmont School. They had played soft ball together. They had eaten lunch in the same lunchroom in the basement of their school. So, what could they have done differently without being obvious about their feelings for one another? They were too young to have shown love, too young to date, too young to show physical affection toward each other. And, if they had, it would have been frowned upon and they would have been disciplined both by their teachers and their parents. And they were too young to be 'paired', which was the pre-engagement period for young couples.

They both quickly walked back to the rehearsal. A few of the other girls had observed Anna and Adam talking quietly together near the water fountain and gave both of them a sly smile. One of them winked at Sarah. Sarah ducked her head and moved onto the risers into her assigned spot, as did Adam. They both knew that their relationship had changed—their young life had changed at the moment they expressed their feelings for each other.

One thing that the other girls in the upper grade choir had apparently not observed was that before Adam and Anna had reached the back stage and the risers. Adam had stopped and had taken Sarah's hand in his. They both stopped briefly and turned to face each other. He then took her other hand, and they stood for just a moment looking into each other's eyes. No words were spoken. Words were not necessary at that moment. They felt a fluttering in their chest that must have been as close to a feeling of love as could have been possible. For that moment—for the first time, they both knew what love, what being in love must be like, that being in love was real, although at age 14 and 15, they were not expected to know what that meant!

The upper and lower grade choirs sang their best. Their many rehearsals had paid off, and the numbers that they sang were sung without error. The play, 'Johnny Appleseed' in which Adam played the lead role went very well. When Adam sang 'The Lord's Been Good to Me', his high tenor voice maintained the correct pitch without breaking down into its newly forming baritone of puberty, it sounded very much like the solo in the Walt Disney version of that same musical play. He received a round of applause when he finished his solo. So, the play went well just as Adam had hoped. He hoped that Sarah was impressed.

After the play had ended, and the children were assembled on stage for their final bow, the applause ended, and Sarah rushed to Adam to tell him how wonderfully she thought he had done. "You sang beautifully, Adam!" she exclaimed. That was all the praise Adam needed to feel satisfied that he had done well.

So, what now? Adam had waited for just the right time, a moment in time—a chance to tell Anna what he had silently held in his heart for more than three years. And, then to find out that she had held similar feelings for him! Such a brief moment of sharing, and in that brief moment of sharing two hearts had joined as one. It was something that neither of them had expected. In that brief moment of time, their lives had changed.

Now, the last day of school performances had concluded, and graduation was to be held tomorrow.

So, what now?

Chapter 8

The next morning the graduation ceremony was to be held at the Cloud County Community Center in Wheatland, Kansas, the nearest town that was large enough to have an auditorium for a celebration of that magnitude. All rural schools in the county would be there for one large ceremony.

The boys wore their Sunday best suits, for most of them their only good suit. A few were store-bought, but most had been hand-sewn by their mother. Adam's suit was purchased at a store in Wheatland, Kansas that sold men's clothing. It was the first Sunday suit that he had ever owned, and in fact the only clothes that had not been made by his mother. In the past, for church he had generally worn a homemade starched white shirt, well pressed dark pants, clean underwear and socks, his shoes freshly shined, wide black suspenders (belts were considered to be 'of the world', so suspenders were required), and his round-brimmed black hat.

Adam's suit was made of soft wool cloth, and the jacket and slacks were dark blue. He had never owned such a finely made garment. Most of the other boys at graduation from Mennonite communities wore suits that their mothers had made for them, and they were not nearly as finely designed as his.

The girls all wore their Sunday best dresses. Some were flowered and others were made of plain color cloth—usually green, dark blue, or another subdued color. Red, lavender, purple or other bright colors were not allowed in this conservative Mennonite culture. All were hand-sewn and freshly ironed. All had the traditional puffed sleeves, collars made of white material, and all dresses were of the same length—the length required by their Mennonite tradition. That is, eight-to-twelve inches above the ankle. Their dresses were heavily starched, and they all wore dark hose that generally matched the color of their dress, plain low heal shoes, and the traditional white cap with straps either hanging loosely about their shoulders, or tied under their chin, depending on how they felt on that day.

The graduation ceremony went well. Nothing extraordinary occurred. After a speech was made by the superintendent of the county schools that the majority of the graduates did not really listen to, each 8th grade graduate from each of the rural schools in their county individually walked across the stage when her or his name was called in order to receive their diploma. They then, one at a time, walked off the stage on the other side and returned to their seat in the auditorium. It was a very solemn occasion. No cheering was allowed, only applause was occasionally heard from non-Mennonite families who had children graduating from other schools in their county.

For Adam, it was a rather sad day, for he felt that he may never see Sarah again, nor she him. Sarah was sitting three seats away from Adam. He looked at her from time to time and felt that she looked beautiful in her flowered dress. Sarah glanced at Adam on occasion during the ceremony and felt that he looked quite handsome in his new navy blue suit.

When the ceremony was over and the graduates and their families gathered outside in front of the Cloud County Community Center, Adam wanted very much to stand near Sarah. She was standing next to her mother and father and her sisters. She glanced up at Adam who was standing nearby. He then caught her eye, and she gave him a fleeting smile and quickly looked down as though she was somewhat embarrassed. Adam hesitantly walked over and stood near her. He was trying to think of something to say when he finally said in a soft voice, "You look very nice, Sarah."

She smiled at him and, in an equally soft voice, replied, "And so do you, Adam. You look extra nice in your blue suit." She again smiled and then looked downward. Adam wanted more than anything at that moment to reach out to her, to take her hands in his and to tell her again how he felt about her—his feelings of love, or whatever his strong feelings were. Perhaps they were not those of true love, but they were feelings so strong that his heart felt like it was going to jump out of his chest whenever he was close to her. He thought, *If that's not love, then I wonder what love is!*

Sarah, in her heart, had similar strong feelings toward Adam. She thought him strong, brave, and handsome. She wanted to be alone with him, and to tell him how she felt— her strong feelings for him. But how that would happen, she did not know. She did not drive a car, but although she was now fifteen years of age and was old enough to have a driver's license. In rural areas of Kansas, a teenager at age 14 was able to apply for a driver's license for running errands and driving to and from school. But she did not have access to a car, nor had she had a driver's examination in order to gain a driver's license. Adam did have a driver's license. He was fifteen years of age and he had a driver's license since his fourteenth birthday.

Adam had access to his father's pickup truck. His family also had a horse and buggy that was used on occasion to drive to church on Sundays. But you didn't need a license to drive one of those. Further, he didn't like driving a horse and buggy. He thought of it as being old-fashioned. He liked driving the pickup truck, but his father told him that it was only to be used for farm work, including hauling harvested grain to the elevator during harvest. He would have to have a very good reason for asking his father if he would allow him to drive over to the Goering farm to visit Sarah. It would have to be an extremely good reason.

The Yoder farm was only four miles away from Sarah's home, so it wouldn't be a long drive. He knew that his father would tease him and try to find his real reason for wanting to see Sarah. So, Adam would have to have a *real* reason for driving over there, other than just to talk to her for a while. But what would that be? He had to have a solid reason—something important. Or did he? Might his father understand Adam's desire to talk to a young woman of their Mennonite Order, someone who he might be later interested in seeing on a social basis and dating? All he could do is ask and see what his father said. After all, he was not asking for the world. He simply wanted to see Sarah to say 'hello' and perhaps remain and talk a little. He just wanted to see her again.

He wished desperately that his family had access to a telephone. After all, Sarah's family had one, and Richie, his nemesis, of course had access to one since his family was 'of the world'. But the Yoder family did not. So, if he drove over to the Goering farm, he would be there without having the opportunity to forewarn Sarah that he was coming over for a visit, and to make sure that she was at home and ready to see him. He would have to risk it!

Chapter 9

So, on Saturday morning he mustered the courage to ask his father if he could drive over to the Goering farm to see Sarah. Since it was only a fourmile drive, he could not think of a reason his father would refuse his request. He approached his father with as much courage as he could muster. His father, whose name was Abraham Yoder, was a muscular man with large hands and a bearded face that appeared to be made of granite. He was working to sharpen the shears of their plow that would be used for plowing their land immediately after grain harvest. He was in the large storage barn where they kept their farm equipment safe from rain so it wouldn't deteriorate from rust and other elements. As he walked toward his father, Adam was rehearsing what he was going to ask.

When he entered the storage barn, his father looked up and said, "Good, I'm glad that you are here Adam. Can you pick up that plow shear by your feet and hold it in the empty slot, the one by my hand, while I rivet it back in place? Nearly without thought, Adam picked up the 50 pound plow shear and placed it neatly in the empty slot on the plow while his father used a heavy hammer to flatten the rivet to hold the plow shear in place. Now, Adam wouldn't have to hold it any longer since it was being held in place by the single rivet. His father then hammered the other four rivets into their proper places. The shear was then snugly mounted in its proper place. Now, only three more plow shears had to be sharpened and replaced for that plow."

Almost automatically, Adam's father looked up and asked, "Did you need something, Adam?"

Adam hesitated for a moment, and then in his most manly voice he asked, "Father, I am wondering if I would be allowed to drive the pickup truck over to the Goering farm. It's only four miles away, and it would only be for a few minutes. May I?" he asked.

His father stopped his work momentarily and looked at Adam. "And why may I ask do you want to drive to the Goering farm?"

Adam now hesitated for an even longer period, "I…I wish to speak to Sarah, their daughter. She and I like to talk, and I would very much like to talk with her for just a little bit of time. May I?"

A sly smile arose on his father's face. He stroked his beard for a moment, and then said through a smile that he could not seem to hide, "And, is there another reason for seeing that young lady? Do you sort of like her? Is she a special young lady in your life?" His father's eyebrows moved up and down in a teasing manner as he began to joke with Adam. "Soooo, you are in love? Is that it? You have found a special lady in your young life?"

"No, it's not that," Adam began to plead. "It's just that we are friends, and we like to talk. I don't even know if she is home since I cannot call her. Oh, I wish that we had a telephone so I could call to see if she is there and wouldn't mind talking a little. I don't like driving over uninvited and imposing on her when she might not even want to see me today!"

"Well," Adam's father hesitated momentarily, and then said, "Well, since it is only four miles away, I suppose you can leave and drive over there. Be sure to tell her father 'Hello' for me if you see him."

Adam was relieved that his father didn't seem to mind if he left for a little while. He was happy that he would be able to make contact with Sarah. He had heard that Richie had been calling her and was trying to make inroads to establish a relationship. Adam felt that it was important to make contact with Sarah so that she would know that he still cared for her.

On Saturday morning, after eating a hearty farm breakfast and telling his father that he was on his way to the Goering farm, Adam jumped into the one pickup truck that his father had purchased and drove down their long driveway to the county road beyond. Turning right, he headed toward the Goering farm to see Sarah. He hoped desperately that she would be there, and that simply 'showing up' to see her would not disturb her too much.

It was only four miles to the Goering farm, but Adam did a lot of thinking as he drove along the bumpy sand and gravel road. He wondered what Sarah would say when he suddenly appeared at the door of their farm house. What would he say? At the moment, he had absolutely no idea.

He had quickly arrived at the driveway of the Yoder farm and made a right turn into their farmyard. The entry to their farm stead was a rather large, graveled oval, with buildings surrounding it. Immediately ahead was a large barn. The hay loft door was open, appearing to be an open mouth ready to accept more hay. Only slightly to the right of the large barn, was a smaller white milk barn. And, immediately to the left were the corrals where some cattle lounged, ready to move out into the pasture. Then, Adam looked over his shoulder to the far right, and there was the back door to the house where Sarah lived.

He sat for a few moments, now wondering why he had driven over to see Sarah when she might not even be here or might not want to see him at this time. He opened the door of the old pickup truck, got out and walked up to the back door of the Goering house.

It was now 10:00 am, so he estimated that everyone would probably be attending to their Saturday duties, and so wouldn't be waking anyone up. The farm seemed quiet. He could hear no activity in or outside of the house.

Well, I guess I'll knock on the door and see if anyone is at home, he thought to himself.

Chapter 10

Adam knocked firmly on the screen door that was about 3 inches from the main wooden door. There was no answer. So, he tried again by knocking firmly three times. At that point, he heard footsteps coming toward the door. His heart began to beat loudly as he waited those few seconds. The door opened, and Mrs. Goering, Sarah's mother greeted him.

"Why, hello Adam," her mother said. "What brings you over her on this Saturday morning?"

"I came to see if Sarah might be home. I just wanted to say 'hello' and see if we could talk a little. She's my good friend, and I thought that it would be nice to see her again since school is out and we have graduated," Adam said almost too rapidly.

"Yes, she is here, Mrs. Goering replied. But, let me see if she feels that she is presentable enough to see you. It may take a few moments if she needs to change her clothes. She's been working around the house helping me with the Saturday house cleaning and laundry. I'll be right back. Please come in and have a seat."

Sarah's mother opened the door and directed Adam through what is called a 'mudroom' in rural America where farmers place their dirty shoes, coats and hats before entering the house. Directly off the mudroom was the kitchen. Adam entered the kitchen and was offered a chair. It was a nice kitchen, friendly looking, and would be a nice place to talk if Sarah was available.

After a few minutes, Sarah entered the kitchen. She was dressed in what obviously were her work cloths. But, to Adam, she was still beautiful no matter what she was wearing. He quickly stood up from the chair as she entered the room and smiled broadly at her.

"Adam! I was not expecting you. I'm not really presentable since I've been helping my mother around the house. I am sure that I look just awful. I'm supposing that I should be saying that it is nice to see you. Can I get you something—a cup of coffee? And, if you'll give me a few minutes, I'll change into something that is more presentable," she said in a rush of words.

"Wait a minute," she paused and thought momentarily and then started over again.

"Let me start over…It's so nice to see you, Adam, but I wish you could have called me to warn me that would be coming over. But, still, it is so nice to see you. I think about you, wondering how you are, and hoping that you're not working too hard."

She paused, caught her breath, and said, "Just give me a few minutes, and I'll be back. We can sit and talk for a while."

Adam, somewhat startled by the rush of words that came from Sarah, indicated that he would be pleased to wait for her. So, she rushed from the room, and was gone. He really didn't know what 'a few minutes' meant in female terms, but he was happy to wait if he had the opportunity to be with Sarah for a little while.

After about 20 minutes, Sarah reentered the kitchen. She was wearing a pretty flowered dress of the Old Order Mennonite tradition, and she was not wearing her white cap, the one with the long flowing ties that draped over her shoulders that she always wore outside of her home. Since she was at home, and with a friend, she didn't feel that she needed to wear it. To Adam, she looked absolutely stunning—beautiful! And he told her so.

"You look beautiful Sarah," Adam said nearly breathlessly as she entered the kitchen. "I would have waited all day just to see you."

"Oh Adam," Sarah responded. "You say the nicest things! But I feel more like having company than I did when you first arrived. I was embarrassed to have you see me like I was."

"But," Adam said in response, "you still look beautiful. I don't care what you wear. You are still the most beautiful girl in this part of the country." Sarah blushed, not knowing what to say in response.

As they sat facing each other at the kitchen table, it was silence that filled the room. Prior to arriving, Adam had neglected to think of things that they could talk about, that would give him something with which to strike up a conversation. So, he fumbled for words, "How have you been, Sarah? I know that it's only been about a month since we graduated, but it seems like a long time. I have missed seeing you."

Sarah looked down at her feet. Her hands were folded in her lap as she said in response, "I have missed seeing you too, Adam. Yes, it does seem like it has been a long time. Has it only been a month? I've been kept busy here mostly doing housework—cleaning and cooking. It gets sort of boring."

She continued, "I wish I could have an adventure of some sort. It doesn't seem fair to me that once we graduate from the 8th grade, we're suddenly kept at home doing the work of adults. We should be allowed to go places, do things, see new places and people. Don't you think so too, Adam?"

Adam, surprised at Sarah's expression of her honest feelings, replied, "I hadn't really thought about it. I guess my strongest desire was to see you. My work on the farm is hard, but if I can see you, everything seems OK."

"But I can see where you are coming from," he continued. "It would be exciting to see new places and meet new people and do different and fun things. Maybe someday we can do those kinds of things together, Sarah. That would be fun. I would really enjoy it!"

Sarah smiled, "I think so too, Adam. It would be fun to do fun things with you. I want to be away from this farm. I feel so confined, so restricted from doing what I want to do." She, in a quiet voice, almost at a whisper so her mother wouldn't hear, "I hate working around the house, doing housework, cooking for hired men. I feel like it isn't what I want to do for the rest of my life."

"Well, when my herd of cattle increases and I become a big cattle rancher, I won't have to spend as much time in the fields or doing regular farm work. If we were together, we could do things and go places, and I wouldn't be as confined to a farm like my father is now," Adam said with confidence.

Their conversation didn't last as long as Adam had anticipated, but he was satisfied that he was able to see Sarah and talk with her for nearly an hour. She was advised by her mother that she still had work to do, and so said goodbye to Adam. As she said it, she looked him in the eye and smiled her lovely smile. Adam wished with all of his heart that he could reach out and hold her for a moment to show her just how much she meant to him. But, with Sarah's mother standing in the kitchen door, he changed his mind. Perhaps it wasn't a prudent thing to do at that moment. He wished that Mrs. Goering hadn't been standing in the doorway.

So, Adam, still feeling the joy of seeing Sarah and talking with her, walked outside to the old pickup truck that he had parked near the back door of the Goering house, and got in. He paused, looking at the house to remember the moments spent with Sarah. Then he started the truck and drove down the driveway to the main road and then home. His only thoughts at the moment were to plan when he could get away from the work on their farm so he could drive back to visit Sarah.

But he wanted access to a telephone so he could call Sarah to see if it was OK to come over to see her. They just had to have a telephone installed. He would speak to his father again and remind him that having a telephone is not simply for social purposes, but also to have access to the rest of the world in case of an emergency!

Chapter 11

Well, Adam's father finally did get ahold of the rural telephone company and scheduled a telephone to be installed in their home. Adam was excited at the prospect of being able to actually make phone calls from their house. He could call anyone he wanted to call if they, too, had their own telephone. Most of all, he was happy that he could call Sarah and wouldn't have to arrive at her house unexpectedly without her prior knowledge or approval just to say 'hello'. In Adam's mind, by this relatively simple upgrade in technology within the Yoder household, things had changed for the better. This is just what he had hoped for.

A week later, he decided that it should be appropriate to call Sarah on their new telephone. Although, he didn't know the Goering's phone number, he decided that he could 'ring up' the telephone operator and ask to be connected to their phone. It was now 10:00 am on Friday. He would ask Sarah if it would be OK to drive over on Sunday afternoon to see her for a little while. He thought that a Sunday afternoon before he had to do his regular afternoon farm chores would be good since no one in their community labored in the fields on Sunday. It was a day of rest from housework and farm labor.

Adam decided that 10:00 am on Friday was an appropriate time to call. Sarah would be up and probably helping her mother around the house. So, he picked up the receiver on their new telephone, turned the dial on the front of the phone one complete turn to signal the operator.

After three rings, he heard a faint click, and the operator's voice came on, "What number please?"

Adam replied in his most confident voice, "The Goering's, on Rural Route 3 please."

The operator paused momentarily, and then returned, "I will ring their number now."

He heard the distant ringing. After it rang several times, he heard a 'click', and a woman's voice said, "Hello?"

Adam responded quickly, "Hello? This is Adam Yoder. I was wondering if Sarah might be there?"

"Yes," the woman was obviously Sarah's mother. "Sarah's in the living room. I'll call her."

He waited a few moments until he heard someone pick up the phone. "Hello Adam? I'm surprised that you called. Where did you find a telephone?"

"We have one now," Adam replied. "It was installed yesterday! I'm calling you to try it out. How do I sound?"

"Perfect," Sarah replied. "You sound perfect! I'm so glad that your parents had a phone installed."

"Yes—me too! Now, I can call you to ask if I can come over, rather than just showing up without your approval."

He paused, and then began again, "Well, the real reason I'm calling is, I'm wondering if it would be OK if I drove over on Sunday afternoon so I could say 'hello' and see you for a little while, I wouldn't stay long. But I miss you when I can't see you."

"I think that would be perfect, Adam. Would around 2:00 pm be OK?"

"Great!" Adam replied. "That's exactly what I was going to suggest. That would be just great!"

The remainder of Friday, and Saturday passed slowly. On Sunday, church was fine as church services go. The sermon was sort of interesting, and Adam only fell asleep once. He saw Sarah sitting with her parents. She turned once to look around and find him, and when she did, and he looked her way, she smiled. To Adam, that made the church service on that day worthwhile.

Sunday dinner was good as always. roast beef with mashed potatoes and good beef gravy, home grown peas that were canned by his mother, yeast rolls with homemade butter, and ice cream for dessert was always a special meal in the Yoder household.

Adam was rather silent through dinner, hoping that 1:45 pm would arrive quickly so he could begin his four mile drive to visit Sarah. At 1:30 pm, he remembered that he had neglected to ask his father if he needed the pickup truck, and if not, could use it. His father said that he didn't need it and wondered why Adam was wanting to use it.

Adam replied, "Oh—I told Sarah that I would drive over to see her for a little bit this afternoon. But I'll be back in time for my chores."

His father smiled a sly and knowing smile, "OK. Have a good visit with your pretty girlfriend. Just be back in time for your Sunday chores."

Adam, without a smile, replied to the 'girlfriend' comment, "Dad, she's not my girlfriend. She's a friend, and that's all!" He had just said an untruth to his father, but he didn't want rumors about him having a girlfriend being spread around the community. It made him feel uncomfortable that people might expect a relationship to blossom when he wasn't sure if it would work out, or if it would last. He felt love when he thought of Sarah but wasn't sure if she felt deep down the same about him.

At 1:45 pm, Adam jumped into the old pickup truck and headed over to the Goering farm to visit Sarah. Even though he had told his father that she was only a friend, in his mind, he wanted her to be more than 'just a friend'. He wanted her to be his steady girlfriend. Whenever he thought of her, his thoughts were of love. He truly felt that he loved her, if what he felt was truly love.

Adam pulled into the Goering's driveway and parked the truck near the back door of their house. But, as he started to open the door to the pickup truck, he suddenly noticed that he had parked near another car that was sitting near the Goering's house. It was a sleek shiny blue car that had bright hubcaps and bright chrome strips along the sides of the car across the doors. The bumpers looked like they had just been shined. They were sparkling.

That certainly would not be a car that the Goering's owned. It was a car that definitely was 'of the world'. Who could own it? Perhaps a visitor from town had come be to say 'hello' to Sarah's mother or father.

Adam finally mustered the courage to leave the old dusty pickup truck and walk up to the back door of the Goering house. Since there was no door bell, he knocked on the door and waited for a response. After a second series of knocks, the back screen door opened and Sarah was standing there looking rather strange. In fact, she looked rather startled to see Adam, and then with a somewhat strained voice said, "Hello Adam—I didn't know that you were coming over. Did you want to see me or my father?"

"I…I came over to see you Sarah," Adam replied. "Don't you remember that we talked by phone on Friday to set a time for today for me to come over to see you? I just wanted to come over to say 'hello' and talk a little. When I don't see you I miss you," the words came pouring from Adam.

Sarah looked down at her feet and stammered slightly, which was unusual for her. She was embarrassed that she had failed to recall that Adam and she had talked on Friday morning.

"I can't talk right now, Adam. It's good to see you, but…I just can't talk right now."

She then hesitated for a moment, as Adam looked at her with a questioning look in his eyes, wondering why she was acting so strangely. Something was definitely wrong. They had a date for this afternoon that he had been looking forward to. It had seemed like an eternity since Friday morning. The time had finally arrived, he had driven over to see her, and now she was acting as though she didn't remember that they were supposed to be together this afternoon. What had happened? Did she not even care that they had a date?

Then after the pause she said, "Richie came over to see me. That's his car that your pickup is sitting next to. I…I…just can't talk right now. I'm sorry that I didn't remember that you were coming over. I really am! But Richie calls me almost every day, or every evening and we talk. He wanted to know if he could come over in his new car to see me this afternoon, and I absolutely forgot that we had a date at this time. I guess I'm just a girl who forgets things," she said with a slightly strained giggle. "I wish you would have called right before you came over this afternoon. Then this embarrassing moment would not have happened."

"But," Adam replied, "We had a date. I didn't think that it would be necessary to call and confirm our time together. I miss you, Sarah, when I don't see you. I truly do! But I guess I'll go. I might call you sometime, but I'm afraid that Richie might be here," he said with some bitterness evidenced in his voice.

"Oh Adam." Sarah was trying desperately to think of something to say. "I really don't know what to say. I want to see you too. But Richie is so persistent in wanting to see me. He is very persuasive. Call me sometime and we'll talk, please?"

Then, Sarah said something that Adam would have never imagined that she would say. She put her hands on her hips and said as though she was judging him, "And Adam, why can't you get a beautiful car like Richie has? Isn't it beautiful? He said that he would give me a ride in it this afternoon. I have never been in such a beautiful car. I never thought I would meet someone who could own one. Our people in this community cannot own cars like that because of our dumb religion. I'll feel like a sinner riding in it, but I don't care."

Adam felt his face beginning to flush, then slowly turning red. He didn't know what to say except that he was sorry that he didn't call her to confirm their date. If he had, he wouldn't be here in this awful situation. He was sorry that he didn't have a fancy car. He was sorry—well, he was sorry for even driving over to the Goering house. And besides that, he had to drive an old dirty pickup truck that he had parked near the beautiful fancy car that was owned by Richie. Adam didn't even own a car! Richie was a year older than Adam, but that shouldn't matter.

Adam was suddenly angry and jealous that Richie was inside of the Yoder house, that he had driven a beautiful car over to their house. He had been calling Sarah on a regular basis in order to establish a relationship with her, and Sarah was apparently allowing him to do that very thing. Why had Sarah allowed him to visit her? Why had she invited him into their house? Why would she do such a thing to him when they already had a date to spend the afternoon together? It seemed a violation of the trust that he felt both of them had established.

He thought that he and Sarah had already established a relationship that in his own mind had begun the final day of their eighth grade behind the stage in the basement of Harmony School by the water fountain. At least he thought that they had established a relationship when they both revealed their feelings for each other on the last day of school when they were backstage. Evidently Sarah, in the meantime, had had a change of heart about her feelings for him, or at least it seemed that way. And now Richie was encroaching on the relationship that he thought he and Sarah shared, and had been invited inside so they could talk. He was actively courting her!

Adam returned to the old pickup that his father had allowed him to drive over to the Yoder farm. The dusty old pickup looked very shabby next to Richie's sleek shiny blue car. *The Johnson family must be well-off,* he thought, *for Richie to be able to drive such a beautiful car.* And Adam did not even have access to a car—any car! It didn't seem fair! All he had access to was an old dusty pickup truck that had rust on the fenders, or a horse-drawn buggy that the Yoder family used on Sunday when they went to church.

Sadly, Adam got into the pickup, started it, and then paused for a moment wondering what to do. He had looked forward to seeing Sarah and talking with her. It would have given them an opportunity to talk and to be together alone for a little while like he had done the week before. But that opportunity was now gone.

Chapter 12

Adam was torn between feeling that he should call Sarah to talk to her to find out about Richie and her feelings about him or calling her to confront her about their own relationship to find out if she had changed her mind. His quandary was that he didn't want to make her angry. But, on the other hand, perhaps he should call her and tell her exactly how he felt, that he felt angry and hurt that their relationship had apparently been sabotaged by Richie. It also angered him that before his father had a telephone installed in their home, Richie had been calling Sarah on a regular basis in an attempt to establish a relationship with her.

On the other hand, perhaps she had felt sorry for Richie, and as a result had invited him over. Perhaps she really did not want to see him, but she somehow felt obligated. Maybe that was it. But, no, she obviously wanted to ride in his beautiful car. But how could he find out? At that point in time, he vowed that he would call her and ask if he could come over so they could talk. He needed some answers!

He slowly turned the pickup around in the large oval entry to the Goering farm and started down their driveway toward the main sand road. He really didn't want to drive home and tell his father what had happened. He just wanted the afternoon to go away, like it never happened. He felt as though his heart had just been broken. He felt ill. His head throbbed. He felt as though he had just been hit in the stomach.

He had never before felt a sense of jealousy. But if this was jealousy, it was awful. If Sarah cared for him as she told him that day when they were backstage before their last day of school performance a year earlier, and a few other times since then, why would Richie be visiting her in their house? Most of all, why was she apparently encouraging him?

Perhaps when he called her, she might explain that Richie had been calling her so much and asking if he could drive over to see her that she felt that she might as well invite him. But she seemed so enamored with his shiny car. Perhaps she was beginning to like Richie. Adam finally decided that the only way he would be able to find out was to call her to set a time to drive over to talk with her.

He drove the four miles back to their farm. As he drove down the bumpy sand and gravel road, he reminded himself of the convenience of having a telephone, and that he would be able to call Sarah to set a time to drive over so they could talk. At least that was one positive happening in his life.

As Adam drove into their farm yard, he was intent on finding his father. As he parked the pickup near the milk barn, he saw his father entering their large round top shed where they parked their larger pieces of farm equipment. Adam followed him in and found him over by one of the tractors. When Adam approached him, his father turned, smiled, and asked Adam how Sarah was. Adam said she was fine, but that a boy was over at their house to visit her—

the boy by the name of Richie Johnson of the Lutheran community, about ten miles north.

"His family is 'of the world', are they not?" his father asked.

"Yes," Adam replied. "Of the world."

"He has been calling Sarah on the telephone so much that either he invited himself over to visit her, or she invited him. I don't know which. But I do know that he has been talking to Sarah quite a bit over the telephone."

Adam's father listened quietly, and then remarked, "I'm surprised that the Goering's allowed the Lutheran boy into their house to visit their daughter. But, on the other hand, he was apparently a guest at their home, so in that respect, I suppose it was OK."

"But," Adam replied, "Sarah seems like it really doesn't matter to her if a boy is from her faith and heritage or not. Maybe she'll allow just anyone to visit her as a potential boyfriend. That, in accordance with our faith and heritage, is not right. What do you think, Dad?"

"Well, after all, she is your special, or apparently possible special person in your life, so I guess that you will have to find out. Go over and talk with her," his father suggested. "See what she has to say for herself."

Adam thought for a moment, and then said, "I just don't know what to think. I was so confused and angry when Sarah told me that Richie was there in their house to visit her, I didn't know what to think! I just kept wondering why she would do that to me since we already had a date set for the afternoon. I thought that she felt that I was someone special in her life. Perhaps you are right. Perhaps she doesn't care if someone special is not from our faith and heritage, that it is OK if he is from 'the world'."

Adam continued, "Richie also has a shiny new car. It is bright blue with shiny chrome on it. It is really good-looking. Sarah kept talking about Richie's shiny car and how she wanted to ride in it. She said that she would feel as though she was sinning to ride in it, but that she really didn't care if she was sinning. I think that he has turned her head so that she has changed somehow. Maybe she has decided to become 'of the world'!"

Adam continued, "At least we have a telephone now so I can call her to set a time so I can drive over to talk. I need to find out a few things. Maybe she has changed. Maybe she does want to become a part of 'the world'. I need to know."

Chapter 13

Adam waited until that evening to call Sarah. After supper at about 7:00 pm, he called. Once again, Sarah's mother answered the phone. He identified himself and asked if Sarah was available. Her mother indicated that she was there and would call her to the phone. In a few moments, she picked up the receiver and said, "Hi Adam! I was wondering if you would call."

"Yes," Adam responded, but without his usual happy voice, "I am wondering if I can come over to see you either this evening or tomorrow evening. I would like to talk with you."

"Not this evening," was her reply. "We have company. But tomorrow evening would be fine."

"Good," said Adam. "How about 7:00 pm. I won't stay long."

"That will be fine, Adam. I am anxious to talk with you also."

When Adam hung the receiver back on their telephone, he wondered aloud what she meant when she said that she was also anxious to talk with him. *What was she saying...or what will she be saying?*

It seemed strange to be going to Sarah's house on a Monday evening. That is not a usual evening for a date with a young lady. But, in Adam's mind, this wasn't going to be a real date. He was going over to talk and find out about where he stood in relation to Richie and Sarah's feelings about him. What he was going to find out might not be what he was hoping for.

Monday evening finally arrived, supper was over and it was 6:30 pm. He had forgotten to ask his father if he could use the pickup truck but hoped that he would be able to use it. His father, when he heard of the purpose of Adam's visit with Sarah agreed that he could use the truck. He knew that it was an important visit that Adam was going to engage in.

At 6:45 pm, Adam jumped into the truck and began the four mile trip to the Goering house. He arrived a little before 7:00 pm, but he wanted to get the discussion with Sarah started. He hoped with all his heart that Richie wouldn't also be there. His new car wasn't sitting in their driveway, so he was satisfied that he wasn't visiting again that evening.

Adam knocked on the back door and Sarah greeted him as though she had been standing at the door waiting for him.

"Come in, Adam," she said. She wasn't smiling as she usually was when she saw him. At this moment, Adam didn't know what to think. He was suddenly dreading the outcome of their discussion.

"Come on into the living room," she said. Adam followed her, and she indicated that he should sit on the couch. He sat at one end, and she on the other, each facing other.

"What did you want to talk about, Adam?" Sarah inquired.

Adam wasn't quite sure how to begin, but he wanted her to know how he felt about essentially being stood up on

Sunday afternoon when they had already set a date for his visit two days earlier.

"Well," Adam began, "I just wanted you to know that my feelings were hurt on Sunday afternoon when I drove over to see you. We had a date for that afternoon at 2:00 pm that we had already set two days earlier. You acted like you didn't even remember that we had a date. You seemed so busy entertaining Richie that you acted as though you didn't care to see me. I just wanted you to know that my feelings were hurt, and that I was angry when I left."

Silence was now filling the living room. Sarah was looking at the floor, and tears were beginning to well up in her eyes.

Adam saw the tears, and quickly said, "I didn't mean to make you sad, Sarah. I didn't mean to make you cry!"

Sarah replied just as quickly, "It's not what you think, Adam. It's just that I am very confused. I like you a lot, Adam. You are a very special young man in my life. We have a history together after being in school all those years, and even after we graduated. But I'm confused. I do care for you. I didn't mean to make you angry on Sunday afternoon. Richie had driven over in his new car, wanting to show it to me. It was so beautiful. I have never in my life seen a more beautiful car. He said that he would give me a ride in it. It was hard for me to refuse, and so I asked him to stay."

"I knew that we had set a date for that afternoon, but something happened to me. That new car and Richie who is 'of the world' suddenly seemed more important to me. Something inside of me was telling me that 'the world' is where I should be—that I am not designed to be confined to the simple life of our Mennonite community, a life of living on a farm, away from the rest of the world."

"That's why I am so confused, Adam. I like you, but I also like what Richie has—a life away from all of this. I know that I am only seventeen years old and shouldn't be making final plans for my life. But it is just how I feel right now. I'm confused. I don't want to ride or drive in a dusty old pickup truck, or the plain cars that we are forced to drive because of our religion. I don't want to live on a farm and do housework for the rest of my life."

Adam was stunned. He didn't know what to say. He wasn't expecting Sarah's outpouring of her feelings. He had no idea that she felt frustrated. He had no idea that she felt the way she did about her life and her future. What could he say? At the moment he couldn't think of anything to say. She, in fact, was telling him that all he might be able to offer her if they ever became married was not what she wanted. She wanted what Richie could give her, which was a life away from what she had experienced since childhood, away from all that Adam could offer her in the future.

"I…I don't know what to say, Sarah," Adam replied quietly. "I came over to talk, and to tell you that I didn't feel good about not seeing you on Sunday afternoon when we had a date set to be together. I wasn't expecting you to tell me all that you have just told me. I had no idea that you wanted a new life away from all that you have known and grown up into—that you would rather have what Richie has. I just don't know what to say! I know that you are only 17 years of age, and we have plenty of time to make decisions about our lives. But you seem to have already made your decision about your future."

Adam continued, "Now I'm really confused! Do you want to see me again—ever? Am I to contact you again? What am I to do, Sarah? I have had feelings of love for you since we were in the 8th grade. I have dreamed of you, perhaps our life together someday, all that we could do together in our life. They have been beautiful dreams. I guess that I am so confused right now that perhaps I should just leave you alone."

"But I've got to tell you, Sarah…I am so jealous of Richie that it hurts deep down inside of me. I feel as though I have been punched in the stomach. You told me once that you had feelings of love for me. Where did those feelings go, Sarah? What made you change? Was it seeing Richie's new car? If that is what made you change, then that is not a good reason. Worldly goods should not change one person's feelings about another person. Something else has changed in you, and I would like to know what it is. You have been my dream come true, Sarah! Again, I have loved you, or had feelings of love for you since we were in the 8th grade together. Right now, Sarah, I feel ill. My feelings are hurt. I hurt!"

"And, if you have nothing more to say, then I feel that I should be leaving, to leave you alone with your change of heart—the change in you. And, if you should change your mind, and would like to see me again, give me a call. I will be here for you whenever you need me. I love you Sarah. I wish with all my heart that you felt the same for me."

Sarah stood, her eyes looking down at her feet, tears welling up into them. She wiped her years away as she looked at Adam, their years together in school and after graduation welling up in her mind. She started to say something, but Adam had already turned and had begun to leave the house, got into the family pickup truck and drove out of the Goering's driveway onto the main road back to their farm without looking back. He was not aware that Sarah had begun to say something as he was leaving.

When Adam arrived back at their farm, he parked the pickup truck in the round top shed with the other pieces of farm equipment and walked to the house. He was stunned, his mind was swimming with more questions than he could handle at the moment. The one question that kept crowding others away was "Why?" Why was Sarah acting as she did this evening? What had happened to her that she would consider leaving all that she knew, all that she had grown up into—her family, the Old Order Mennonite way of life, all that she knew, and her feelings about him?

He didn't feel like going to bed and sleeping. He was hurt deeply. He simply felt ill. He had a strong feeling that he may never hear from Sarah again. But he knew that his feelings for her—his love for her would never die!

Chapter 14

Two years passed. Both Adam and Sarah were now nineteen years of age, and Adam had not seen Sarah for nearly a year, not even at church on Sundays. He wondered where she might be. Prior to that time, they had talked occasionally, but he also knew that Richie had been over to see her. When he had called her home, both her mother and father many times told him that they did not know where she was. That was strange since they were such a close-knit family.

In spite of his feelings of rejection, he could not release his dream, still, that was to establish a relationship with Sarah, and perhaps marry her. His dream, further, was to settle down on a farm, raise cattle, and have a family with a lovely wife, who he dreamed would be Sarah. He simply could not give up this dream.

During those two years, Adam had earned enough money through the small salary that his father had paid him for his help on their 1280 acre farm to buy a good car of his own. Although it was quite used, it did run well. It wasn't pretty. It wasn't good-looking like those of Richie, but rather a dull dark blue color with hubcaps removed and as little chrome as possible. In accordance with his family's conservative Mennonite doctrine of the Old Order Aldeman

Mennonite, of not becoming part of 'the world', he had removed the shiny hubcaps, and all of the chrome that he could from that plain four door 1950 Dodge sedan.

Adam had also taken a sizable amount of the salary he had been paid by his father to start his own small herd of Black Angus beef cattle. He had driven the old pickup truck to the Cloud County Sale Barn located at the west edge of Wheatland, Kansas, and used $600 to buy six head of very young Black Angus steers, that when fed and fattened would be sold at that same sale barn, hopefully for a profit. With the potential profit, he hoped to purchase a larger herd in order to continue building toward a sizable herd to begin his life's occupation of raising and selling high grade beef cattle.

His fear was that his dreams were beyond potential reality. Who was *he* to dream of marrying Sarah? She was not making any attempt to contact him. It was as though he didn't exist in her life anymore. In fact, the Sunday a week ago, he had seen her at church with Richie. Now, why would she bring someone 'of the world' to their Aldeman Mennonite Church? He wondered what her parents had said about it. He thought that they should be angry and embarrassed. But he didn't see her parents. Were they even there? Were they so embarrassed that they did not go to church that Sunday? Adam did know that if Sarah dated or married a non-Old Order Mennonite, she nor her mate would be invited to family gatherings. And if they became married, her parents would not be able to attend their marriage ceremony. And for all other purposes that couple would no longer exist.

What was Sarah thinking? Why would she essentially flaunt the beliefs of their church and bring someone 'of the world', as though she was dating him? Was she dating Richie? Was she committed to him? Were they paired, which would mean that they were in essence 'pre-engaged'?

Why was she doing this to him and to her parents? Adam saw members of their church whispering to each other as they saw Richie and Sarah together driving up to the church in his shiny blue car with shiny hubcaps, and chrome along the sides. When Sarah got out of the car, she grabbed Richie by his arm, and walked with her nose in the air and a smile on her face as though she was showing off, as though she didn't care what people thought.

It just wasn't like her. She had always been such a nice, lovely girl who Adam had looked up to—who he wanted to be with more than anything else.

Adam approached Sarah just as church let out for the day to say 'Hello'. He had no more than opened his mouth to say it when she said with an air of what appeared to be artificial elegance, "Did you see Richie's car? Isn't it beautiful? I just love riding in it. Now, he's going to let me drive it too," she said arrogantly, and then walked off. Adam remained standing where he had intended to say 'Hello', but now with his mouth open, wondering what had just happened to the lovely, gentle, and kind young woman named Sarah? What had happened to her during the two years they had not been together? She apparently had become someone he did not know anymore.

Chapter 15

Adam heard via the grape vine of the Wheatland Mennonite Church that Sarah was passed being paired to Richie Johnson and was engaged to him. She was forsaking her relationship with her family and her church. Within the doctrine of the Aldeman Mennonite Order, becoming engaged or married to someone who was not a member of their Old Order Mennonite would result in revocation of membership in their church, and to be disowned, or at least shunned, from one's family. That meant in essence that she no longer avowed membership within the religion into which she had been born and raised and would no longer be considered a member of her family.

If she became married to the person 'of the world', it meant that they as a couple would not be invited to attend any family gatherings on the bride's side from that time on, nor would the family participate in or attend the wedding ceremony. Therefore, her father would not be able to walk with her down the aisle during the ceremony, nor would any member of her family be able to participate in the ceremony in any way, nor, in fact, even attend the ceremony. That was true punishment—to be banned or shunned from one's family.

Adam felt badly for Sarah. Why had she done this to herself? She must be truly in love or must have simply strayed from her religious faith and her family. Or was she simply rebelling. He was sure that her family felt terrible about this situation. But Sarah was of age now at age 19, and could manage her life as she saw fit to do so.

To his dismay, Adam realized that this was the end of what he had hoped for. His dreams of being with Sarah someday in marriage, raising a family, living on their farm together as husband and wife were destroyed. When he heard that the marriage had occurred, and Richie and Sarah were now husband and wife, Adam hurt more than he could have ever imagined. He had not realized that the pain of rejection could hurt so deeply.

She had married against her parent's wishes, and those of her Mennonite faith and doctrine. Adam silently and with sad determination realized all too well that Sarah was gone out of his life, out of her family, their church, and their community. If he now dared enter into a relationship with a young woman, he would have to search for someone else. He simply felt empty down into the pit of his stomach. He felt ill. Sarah was all that he had dreamed of. She was his ideal, the young woman he had longed for and for whom he felt love. He felt a heavy weight in the pit of his stomach.

But now, he must go on with his life. He would try to forget Sarah. She was gone. She had made her decision to leave all that she knew, her church and her family, and move into another form of life. He hoped that she would be happy, but he could not believe that she actually could be. He was sure that her family was grieving. They had lost their daughter. She was no longer considered a member of her family. Her family did not even know where she was living!

Adam strongly believed that soon, after the newness of her rebellion and her new life away from all that she had known since childhood had faded, Sarah would begin to grieve the loss of her family.

Her parents, nor any other member of her family had attended Sarah's wedding. Adam felt sorry for her. But she had chosen the circumstance she now found herself in when she accepted Richie's marriage proposal.

Adam had not been able to imagine why Sarah would fall in love with Richie. He was the antithesis of her—the complete opposite. Perhaps it was because he was so different, essentially from another world that was not theirs that attracted her and her feelings of rebellion against everything she had known. He drove a flashy car, went to high school and then into college. He had taken Sarah with him into another world, away from their community and the way of life of her family, away from their faith and Mennonite doctrine. She seemed to have fallen in love with a different world, a different way of life, a life in 'the world', away from all that she knew.

What had she been thinking when she said 'Yes' to Richie's proposal of marriage? How did she tell her parents? Had she somehow been brainwashed by him? Was she truly herself when she accepted his proposal of marriage? Why had she said 'Yes'? Why? What had happened to her?

Those were among the many questions that Adam continued to ask himself. He knew that he would probably never find the answers. Perhaps, if he talked with her parents. Perhaps they would have insights into his questions, the questions that would give him some insights on 'Why'?

Chapter 16

Yes—that is what he would do. He would talk to her parents to see if they had answers to his questions. He wasn't sure if it would do any good if he did find answers to his questions, but he would at least know more than he did now.

So, he decided that he would call Sarah's home to set an appointment with her parents, to ask if they knew why she had strayed away from her family and church. His only hesitation was that by asking 'why', he may be opening wounds that her parents would not want to talk about. After all, in the eyes of her parents, Sarah no longer existed. In becoming a part 'of the world', she had left her family, her Mennonite heritage, her personal and family heritage, and had in a sense was no longer a part of their family. The mourning of her parents may still be fresh, and so perhaps it would be unkind to open the door into their mourning by asking questions. It would probably be best to wait for a few more weeks before contacting them.

After a few weeks had passed, he called the Goering's number on the telephone. Sarah's mother answered with a pleasant, "Hello?"

Adam began, "Hello Mrs. Yoder. This is Adam Yoder. As you know, I am Joseph Yoder's son and Sarah's friend."

"Oh yes, Adam. Of course I know you. You have been a friend of Sarah's who was once our daughter. What can I do for you?"

Adam replied, "Well—I was wondering if I might come to your house for a moment sometime soon. I have a question that you might be able to answer."

"Why certainly. Anytime, Adam. Come on over any time. It seems as though I am always here."

"May I drive over now? It only takes about 10 minutes to drive to your house."

"That will be just fine Adam. Come right on over," was Mrs. Goering's reply.

Adam found his father and asked if he needed him at the moment. If not, he would be right back. He had an errand to run. His father didn't need him right at that time, so Adam jumped in his own car, the 1950 Dodge, and drove to the Goering farm. As he drove into their driveway and the large gravel entry to their farm, he recalled the day he had driven over hoping to see Sarah to talk for a little while. He remembered the shiny blue car that belonged to Richie, and how his heart felt as though it had dropped down to his toes when Sarah said that he was in their house to visit her. He tried to avoid those memories, but they still seemed fresh in his mind, and probably would for some time.

He got out of his car, walked up to the back door of the Yoder home and since there was no doorbell, he knocked. Doorbells were something 'of the world' that those of the Aldeman Mennonite Order did not need or even seem to desire.

Sarah's mother came to the door and invited Adam into their house. He remembered when he in the past had happy moments in their kitchen with Sarah, and sad moments with her in their living room. But he was always impressed with the neatness of their home. It was very tidy, and the furniture, lamps, curtains and all were pretty but still plain—nothing fancy, but clean and well kept.

She asked Adam to be seated and asked if he would like something to drink. He said that he didn't need anything at the moment. Mrs. Yoder hurried into the kitchen and brought both of them a slice of poppy seed roll. Poppy seed rolls in their German/Prussian tradition were thin and flaky rolls that were filled with a thick delicious poppy seed mixture that was so good that it seemed to be something out of this world! Adam gladly accepted one of the rolls. They sat momentarily and enjoyed the delicious texture and sweetness of the rolls, while Mrs. Yoder waited for Adam to tell her why he was there—the question he had mentioned that he wanted to ask.

Finally, Adam mustered the courage to ask his question. "Mrs. Yoder—as you might know, or might have guessed, I have admired Sarah for a number of years. She has been sort of my image of an ideal young woman, and I had admired and cared very much for her, but always, it seemed it was always from afar. I told her once right before we graduated from eighth grade how I felt, that I had feelings of what I felt were love for her, and she confessed that she likewise had similar feelings for me. Even though we were very young at that time, I felt that at the right time in our lives, we could begin dating, and seeing each other on a social basis. Again, even at that young age I felt that I was in love. But I doubt if I really knew what love was." Adam smiled, blushed and looked down at his feet as a result of that confession.

Mrs. Goering smiled and then said, "I thought so, Adam. I had thought that there was something special between you and Sarah. She talked about you in the evenings at supper and how she admired you. I had secretly hoped that someday when the time was right, you two would begin to see each other on a more 'social' basis, if that is what you call it."

"I, too, was hoping for that to happen," Adam replied.

He continued, rather hesitantly at the beginning, "But, recently, I was sickened to hear that she had been seeing the young man by the name of Richie Johnson who is 'of the world', and then married him. I simply could not imagine that Sarah would do such a thing. I kept asking myself *Why? Why would she do that?*

"The question that I brought with me when I drove over to see you, Mrs. Goering, is that I am wondering if you might know what happened to her that would cause her fall in love with a young man of the world and had in essence given up her family and her heritage. I will confess that I had actually made plans in my own mind that Sarah and I would someday get together, and that we would see each other as boyfriend and girlfriend."

Adam blushed once again when he confessed all of that to her. But he wanted Sarah's mother to know that he had, in his own mind, made plans for his and Sarah's future together.

Mrs. Yoder had stopped eating her poppy seed roll, and tears began rolling down her cheeks. She slowly struggled to say, "This has been a true tragedy in our family, Adam, as she wiped tears from her eyes and cheeks. We do not know what happened to her. She suddenly changed to be a different person than we had known as she was growing up. She became bitter and resentful of her heritage, the conservative Old Order Mennonite life, of being confined to our farm, of housework, of the prospects for her future. We do not know what happened that brought these feelings about. She stopped talking to us. All she wanted to do was drive around with that boy Richie in his new car. It has been a terrible time for our family, Adam."

She paused, wiped more tears from her eyes, and began again, "Sarah, as you might suspect, is no longer a member of our family. She was shunned as a member of our family the day she became engaged, and then became married to that young man who is 'of the world'. We are no longer communicating with her and will not as long as she is with him. We simply do not know what happened to her that made her abandon her family and her Mennonite doctrine and heritage. We simply do not know. I am sorry that you drove over here only to hear that. I wish—oh…I do wish that if she was going to fall in love with someone, that it would have been someone like you, Adam. That is all I know. I really do not want to talk about it anymore but thank you for coming over."

Adam thanked her for taking the time to meet with him, and for the delicious poppy seed roll, and then he quietly left. He now knew little more than he knew when he drove over to speak with Sarah's mother, except that her mother, and he was sure also her father, were very sad that Sarah had married someone who was not of their faith and Mennonite heritage. She apparently did not know why

Sarah had left her family and her church, and was just as mystified as Adam was. 'Why'? is always a difficult question when the person who has the answer is not there to respond to it.

Well—it was over. Sarah was gone. In the pit of his stomach, Adam felt a pain of emptiness that simply would not go away.

He did not know where she was at this time. Was she happy? Was she well? What had happened in her life to cause her to give up her life with her family and her church, and to give up the feelings of caring that she apparently had at one time for Adam?

Chapter 17

Adam drove down the long driveway of the Goering farm, and headed for home. He supposed that he should tell his father what had happened to the one love he had experienced in his young life. Maybe his father, with his words of wisdom, would make him feel better, or give him hope for his future.

The four miles back to the Yoder farm went by quickly, and as he pulled into their driveway he saw his father walking out to the milk barn. Adam parked his car and followed his father into the coolness of the milk parlor where their cows were milked twice a day. As he approached his father, his father took the initiative to begin the conversation.

He asked, "How are the Goering's? I heard through the grapevine that Sarah has essentially run away from home and married a young man 'of the world'. Have they heard anything from her—anything at all? Have you heard anything from her? I thought that you and she had something going on between you two. Or was that wishful thinking on your part? From what I hear, she just vanished with the young man. They think she is rebelling—that she has decided that his world, the world of flashy cars and nice clothes is better than ours."

Adam was quiet for a moment, trying to think of what to say. He finally began, "I just went to see Sarah's mother to see if she had any information about her. All she said is that they are very sad. Her mother was crying. They do not know what prompted Sarah to do what she did, to essentially run away and leave her family and her heritage."

"She said that Sarah is now no longer a member of their family, and that as long as she is married to Richie who is 'of the world', she is beyond being shunned. She is essentially dead. They are very sad, wondering where she is, and what she is doing. I would imagine that her father would like to search for her, but from what her mother has gathered, he has no idea where to begin such a search."

As Adam continued, he began pouring out his thoughts to his father who listened quietly. "Father, I had real plans for Sarah and me. I thought that she cared as deeply for me as I cared for her. She even told me so. As you know, I have started my cattle business, or at least I now have a small herd, and my plans were that as I built up that business, and when I felt secure about my financial future, I would begin dating Sarah, and then I was hoping that we would become 'paired' (a pre-engagement period that was a part of the ritual of courtship of their Alderman Mennonite heritage), and then hopefully eventually become engaged and then married. I was also hoping that you and I could build a house near yours and mother's house so Sarah and I could live there, and I could continue to farm and increase my cattle herd so that eventually I could become financially independent through my cattle enterprise."

He continued, "That's what I had hoped for Sarah and me. But now it is gone! With Sarah doing what she did, my dream is gone. I'm really at a loss for what to do!"

"Adam, your dream of you and Sarah may be gone, but your dream of a house and your cattle enterprise is not," his father replied. "Keep your dream close to your heart, Adam, and another 'Sarah' will eventually come along. There are many nice young women out there who are faithful to our Mennonite heritage and will make a wonderful mate for you."

Joseph Yoder continued, "And, just remember Adam, the young woman who you find doesn't have to be a member of our identical Alderman Mennonite Order, but perhaps one that is similar. We will bring her into the fold of our family, and you will find love as you have never experienced it before. Wait and see. It will happen!" His father smiled, then put his arm around Adam's shoulders, and squeezed him in a reassuring manner.

Adam looked at his father and knew that he was right. Perhaps something good would happen someday soon. He tried very hard to smile, but at that time he simply couldn't force one. His father was smiling in a reassuring way, and all that Adam could do was to look down sadly but knew that his father was right.

Chapter 18

Time passed, and Adam threw himself into the work of their farm. One thousand two hundred and eighty acres was the largest farm in Cloud County and required a great deal of work getting the soil ready for planting wheat that was their primary crop for that part of the country. Although they grew other crops on that large acreage, wheat was their staple crop. Wheat was called a 'dry weather crop', since it could withstand growing seasons with little rain, but still produce well. To maintain a farm that was the size of theirs, they needed at least one staple crop, one that could withstand both wet and dry growing years.

Adam's father did not want to hire other farm hands unless he absolutely had to, so Adam was depended on to maintain the labor of at least two men. That meant long hours in the fields plowing, disking, and other forms of field work, wheat harvest, and cutting and baling hay for his cattle. It also meant the dangerous job of running the 'chopper' for harvesting corn and cane sorghum that was blown into their silo so that it would ferment for eventual feeding to their dairy cows and Adam's beef cattle especially during the long winters. Of course, Adam and his father shared the workload, but it still required day after day of long hours in the hot sun for both during the summer.

When Adam was in their fields on the tractor he was assigned to drive, listening hour after hour to the drone of the diesel engine, his thoughts wandered. Those long hours gave him a great deal of time to think, compose songs, write stories in his mind, and dream of his future. His thoughts would sometimes drift to those of Sarah, wondering where she was, what she was doing, what she was thinking, wondering if she ever thought of him. He tried not to think of her, but the problem was, the more he tried not to think of her, the more she remained in his thoughts.

So, he would compose more songs, and write more stories in his mind. However, somehow, the songs became love songs, and the stories inevitably became stories of unrequited love—stories in which the one who was loved would for some reason reject the one who loved. He tried to compose happy love stories, but those did not seem to come to mind. So, he would compose adventure stories, and those would sometimes get his mind off Sarah.

At night after he had showered the dirt and grime from his work in the fields, and would climb up the thirteen stair steps to his room on the second floor of their 1864 vintage farm house and then crawl into his soft bed. He was usually so tired that he did not think of anything before falling to sleep.

On Sundays, they did not work in the fields. That day involved church and was a day of rest. So, on Sunday night when he would crawl into bed, his thoughts would turn to Sarah. It frustrated him that he could not get her out of his mind.

Why could he not forget her? She was gone. She did not even exist in the minds of her parents or their church. So, why did she live so well in his mind? Adam tried to remove her from his thoughts. But she simply would not leave. She seemed to have left an indelible image in his brain—the image of her loveliness, her grace, her face, and what she told him backstage just before their eighth grade last day of school musical performance when she said that she cared for him—she truly cared for him, wanted to be with him, and had the same feelings about him as he did about her. Those were feelings of love, or what they thought was love.

So, what was he to do? He went to church each Sunday, and to Youth Group for young people ages 15 through 20 years that was held on Sunday evenings in the basement of the Wheatland Mennonite Church. That group met each Sunday evening at 7:00 pm. They sang hymns, prayed, and either brought in entertainment of some sort, or they engaged in games that involved knowledge of the bible, vocabulary games, games involving U.S. history, and others. The girls were of course all of their Mennonite Order, all dressed the same, and seemed for some reason to mostly look the same—same clothes, same shoes, same hair. He didn't see one of them who might in the least bit be attractive to him. They all seemed to like him, wanting to sit next to him during their youth meetings. Since he was among the older more mature males who attended those meetings, at age 19 years, he supposed that was the reason they wanted to sit with him.

Chapter 19

One week Adam decided to attend the Sunday evening Youth Group at a different Mennonite church that was located at the far end of Cloud County. It was not of the conservative Aldeman Mennonite Order but was a slightly more modern denomination called General Conference Mennonite. The church's name was the Little River Mennonite Church. The next Sunday evening when he entered the room where the Youth Group met at that church, he was surprised to see the young men wearing blue jeans and colored shirts. Many wore tennis shoes. Most of the young women were wearing slacks or blue jeans and blouses, with slippers or sneakers on their feet. Most even wore makeup including lipstick and rouge, and their hair was styled in very attractive ways.

Adam had no idea that there was a Mennonite Order that allowed those types of dress for young men and women. His plain handmade pants and shirt that had no collar, along with his plain round brim hat and rough shoes looked very much out of place in comparison with what the others were wearing. He was somewhat embarrassed. But the others in attendance at the gathering welcomed him, and wondered where he came from. He explained that he was from the Aldeman Mennonite Order, the Wheatland Old Order

Mennonite Church located at the other end of the county. And with that they understood the difference in manner of appearance.

The girls in attendance at the Youth Group were nice. Some of them he felt were quite pretty, but he felt that perhaps the prettiness was partly due to the fact that they were wearing makeup, and they were not wearing the traditional white cap of the young women of his Mennonite Order. In fact, their hair seemed to be styled in various pretty ways—some long and straight, others short and curly.

Adam remained there for a while, but he began to feel rather uncomfortable in attending a gathering of young men and women who seemed to be 'of the world' rather than of the traditional conservative Mennonite Order to which he belonged. After a while, he left and drove back to their farm. It was a sixty-three mile drive, so he arrived home later than his parents were expecting. But, at nearly twenty years of age, however, they had expected him to begin to live a life of his own, and so they didn't seem really worried.

He told his parents about the Youth Group he had attended at the Little River Mennonite Church, how they were dressed, and the fact that they seemed to be more akin to those 'of the world' that he was not used to. He said that he had felt somewhat uncomfortable being there, particularly regarding how he was dressed as compared to them. He did not realize that there was that much difference between the Aldeman Mennonite Order and the General Conference Mennonites.

In any event, he realized that he felt more comfortable among his own people. Even though the young women in his Wheatland Mennonite Church were plain in their appearance, no lip stick or rouge, no slacks or blouses, he felt more comfortable being with them. Even though he felt comfortable being with them and talking with them, to him none of them seemed attractive.

Then one Sunday evening, one of the young women in their Youth Group brought her cousin with her whose name was Catherine. Catherine was a very attractive young woman—rather tall, stately, carried herself perfectly, possessed pretty blond hair that seemed to have a natural curl that was evident even while wearing the traditional white cap, and had beautiful blue eyes. Her lips were full and with a natural rose tint that made them very appealing, almost as though she was wearing lip rouge. She still wore the plain long ankle length dress of the Aldeman Mennonite Order along with the white cap that was perched daintily on the back of her pretty head.

Adam was stunned when he saw her. He mustered a strained 'Hello' and smiled. She turned, smiled and returned the greeting in a rather non-committal manner. He wasn't sure if she meant it or not, or rather as the return of a greeting out of habit. It seemed rather abrupt.

Not willing to give up, he tried during the remainder of the evening to strike up a conversation with Catherine, but to no avail. She essentially ignored him. She smiled occasionally, but it seemed to be forced. She definitely did not seem interested in getting to know him.

He even heard her cousin Evelyn tell Catherine quickly and quietly that he would like to meet her. So, during the social portion of the evening, Evelyn brought Catherine over to where Adam was standing so she could introduce her to him. Adam smiled during the introduction, as did

Catherine. They both nodded to acknowledge their introductions, and Adam said with enthusiasm, "It is very nice to meet you, Catherine," stressing the 'very' to let her know that he was extremely happy to meet her.

She returned the greeting, "And, it is very nice to meet you, Adam. Evelyn has said some very nice things about you." Adam was flattered and hoped that it might be the beginning of something special with this beautiful young woman. But that feeling of hope was soon shattered.

"So," she continued in what seemed to be an interrogating manner, "I was told by Evelyn that you are a cattleman, that you are raising cattle on your farm? How many head of cattle do you currently own?"

Adam wasn't expecting a question that probed his business life and hesitated to answer since he was just starting out in the cattle business and did not own very many. But he innocently answered her question anyway, "I'm just getting started in the cattle business since most of what we do on our farm involves wheat and other grains. I intend to concentrate on cattle exclusively. That seems to be where the money is. Right now, I have twelve head in my herd, and as soon as they are ready for market, I'll sell those and buy more. So, next year at this time, I should have around twenty head of Black Angus steers," he said proudly.

"Oh?" she asked. "Only twelve head of cattle? And you call yourself a cattleman?" she said in a rather demeaning manner.

"Well, I hope to be a big cattleman eventually. I'm just getting started," he defended himself.

Catherine turned and started to walk away, but said as she left, "Let me know when you are a true cattleman, and I might be interested in getting to know you better." And she walked briskly away, swishing her dress, her nose in the air.

Evelyn, the cousin who brought her to the Youth Group stood with her mouth open as Catherine walked away, wondering what had just happened. She raised her shoulders and spread her arms to indicate to Adam that she did not know what was going on with Catherine. Adam recognized Evelyn's gesture of frustration and nodded to her in an affirming manner. Evelyn walked over to where Adam was standing and apologized for her cousin's actions. As she was apologizing, she recognized Adam's deflated look and then decided to wait before saying more. Adam was, indeed, deflated. He felt genuinely insulted by Catherine's actions.

He thought to himself, *She may be pretty, but she certainly does not seem to be very nice.* He was depressed and somewhat angry as a result of her obvious demeaning response to his answers to her questions. *She must think of herself as being very important*, Adam thought. *She must feel that she is more important than she really is.* He decided at that moment that Catherine was not worth trying to get to know. And, even though she might be attractive physically, she was not attractive as a person!

There must be young women somewhere out there who are both attractive and nice! he thought. *But where are they?* Sarah, he felt, had cared very much for him, but then she left him for a young man 'of the world' and married him! Tonight, he had met a very pretty young woman of his

Mennonite Order who, upon meeting him, rejected him almost immediately!

Something was wrong! Where were all the young women who are not only attractive but also good and kind, and who he would enjoy being with, who he could genuinely care for because of their kindness and their loving nature, and would like and care for him in return? *Where are they?* he wondered.

Once again, he got into his car and drove back to the farm. He went up to his room and began to get ready for bed. It was late, and he had, in essence, wasted an evening trying to get to know an attractive young woman who was apparently of their same Mennonite Order, but to no avail. She was obviously looking for someone who could support her in the manner to which she would like to become accustomed. Adam was not looking for someone like that. No matter how successful he became in the cattle business, he did not want to be with a woman who cared only for the money he made. He dreamed of being with a woman who cared for him, who loved him for who he is, not for what he has, and who he could love without boundaries, and with all of his heart.

He continued to get ready for bed. It was Sunday night, and he had to be ready for a full day of work in the morning. So, he climbed down the thirteen steps of the stairway and to the bathroom on the first floor of their old house to take a shower, brush his teeth, and then climb back up the long stairway to his second story bedroom.

After climbing the long stairway and walking into his bedroom, Adam climbed into his big double bed and began to drift off to sleep. As occurred all too often, his thoughts once again turned to Sarah. His mind seemed not to want to let go of her. He didn't intend to think of her right then, but his thoughts simply moved in her direction. What was she doing? Where was she? Did she ever think of him? Why did she go away with someone who seemed to him to be a stranger—a man 'of the world', and marry him? It simply did not make sense.

The next morning, he slowly got out of his bed, dressed in his everyday work clothes, and walked downstairs to the bathroom on the first floor to brush his teeth, rinse his face, shave around the Mennonite beard that he was starting to grow around his chin, and comb his thick brown hair. The beard that he was cultivating was that of the typical conservative Old Order Mennonite—no mustache since that was considered 'of the world', and otherwise a closely trimmed beard around the jaw and chin. As he looked at himself in the mirror, he realized that he needed a haircut. His hair was hanging over his ears, and down over the back of his shirt collar. His mother was the barber of the family since they did not go to barbers in town. To do that would be too much akin to being 'of the world', and not their simple life of the Aldeman Mennonite Order.

He then went out to complete the morning chores for which he was responsible. Those included throwing down eight bales of hay from the haymow that was located within the upper floor of the large old barn. The alfalfa hay was for the Holstein milk cows and his twelve head of Black Angus steers. He then began feeding the six baby calves that had recently been born from the milk cows, and fed the one Holstein bull that was kept in a separate pen. He also had to make sure that all of the stock had plenty of water.

After completing the chores, he would return to their farm house for a sizable breakfast of hot wheat cereal that was made from wheat kernels that they had harvested the year before, two poached eggs from the dozen chickens his mother took care of so that they would have a steady supply of eggs for eating and cooking, three pieces of home cured bacon, and two thick slices of homemade wheat bread that his mother had baked, along with homemade grape jam. Everything was grown or made on their farm and prepared by Adam's mother. If possible, nothing was bought in stores. It was nutritious, and all was homemade. Perhaps that was why Adam had continued to maintain his wholesome appearance and his immaculate state of health.

Chapter 20

Three months went by. It was now more than two years since he had seen Sarah. His life was as usual, consisting of chores, working in the fields, making sure that his twelve head of Black Angus steers were well fed so that they would be ready for market in about three more months. He went to church on Sundays, and some of the few remaining Youth Group meetings on Sunday evenings that he would be permitted to attend. He was now twenty-one years of age, and therefore he had moved beyond the age of those for whom the gathering of young people had been intended, that is age twenty as the oldest.

It was Sunday morning. After completing his chores and eating breakfast, he dressed in his only homemade suit, no tie of course since that was considered 'of the world', no shirt collar for the same reason, his best shoes and socks, and his best round-brimmed hat that was consistent with their Mennonite Order. He then went to the corral and called for Ginger, their beautiful red Morgan trotter so he could harness and hitch her to their family buggy that they used to take them to church on Sunday mornings. Ginger was of the Standard Bred lineage, the same breed of horse that is used world-wide for carriage pulling. They had a certain style that people liked with a little Thoroughbred and Morgan heritage. Ginger was fifteen hands tall and was always ready to pull their buggy. Trotting came rather naturally to that breed of horse. They held their heads high and lifted their hooves with style as they trotted down the road. That was one of the few luxuries that their Older Order Mennonite heritage had been permitted through the years.

They could have driven Adam's 1950 Dodge, but most people who attended their church drove horses and buggies on Sunday to church. It had become a tradition that most did not want to break. It brought them back to their roots, so to speak. Of course, the Yoders owned their pickup truck, but it did not seat three people comfortably, and they did not own a family car like some in their community. For whatever reason, they did not see a reason to have two cars and a pickup truck. Perhaps someday they would invest in a family car, but for some reason that had not become important up to this point in their life.

While Adam was preparing the horse and buggy for the five-mile trip to church, his thoughts once again were transported to his dream of meeting a young woman from his family's Mennonite Order who would be the one who he would get to know as a potential mate. He wished that he would arrive at their church on a Sunday morning and see her there waiting for him. Ah…such a dream that he wished somehow would become a reality.

But that dream seemed nearly impossible since there didn't seem to be any new families moving into their area of the state, let alone the county where their church was located. He knew that he would know if someone moved into their area of the state. If that happened, the word would spread quickly throughout their community.

As soon as Adam had hitched Ginger to the buggy, she was ready to go. She was chomping at the bit of the bridle and was prancing gaily. Adam had a difficult time holding her back. He quickly tied her to a fence post near the back door of their farm house and ran into the kitchen to tell his mother and father that Ginger was ready to go.

When everyone was settled in the two seated buggy, Adam released Ginger and she eagerly trotted down their driveway and onto the main road. The five miles to the Wheatland Mennonite Church was a pleasant drive on a cool Sunday morning. The birds were singing from the trees that lined the road, and the regular clip-clop cadence of the hooves of the trotting horse against the hard packed road nearly lulled everyone to sleep. The trip was such a pleasant one that the simple aesthetic nature of the trip was one of the reasons that they continued to use a horse and buggy for the ride to church and back each Sunday. It was simply too nice to give up.

The Yoder family pulled up to the front of the church building, and Adam's parents stepped out of the buggy. Adam then drove Ginger and the buggy over to the side of the church where the other horses and buggies were parked. After allowing Ginger to drink her fill at the horse watering trough, and parking her and the buggy alongside the other horses, Adam pulled a feed bag from the back of the buggy and put enough corn mixture in it to keep Ginger happy for a while during the church service.

Adam then walked to the front of the church and entered. He searched for his parents and could not locate them for a moment. He spotted them and quietly walked down the side isle where his mother and father were seated.

His mother scooted over enough for him to be seated next to her. The service had not yet begun, so Adam spent some time looking around at all of the people who were in attendance. Since the women, both younger and older and depending on their age and marital status wore either white or black bonnets or white, black or navy blue caps with long straps that hung over their shoulders or were tied under their chin, it was difficult to tell one from the other from where he sat in the congregation. They mostly looked the same. The men wore nothing on their heads while in church, so he could recognize most of them.

As he relaxed and looked around at the people in the congregation, he spotted one woman who held his attention. She was apparently younger than others sitting around her, and she was wearing a white cap with long strap ties that hung about her shoulders. Her profile was what caught his attention. She looked very familiar, but at that angle he couldn't quite see her well enough to tell who it was. He spent the next few minutes trying his best to move a little into a better position to see who it was. His position in their pew was such that he finally gave up because of the advice given to him by his mother who whispered for him to stop moving around in his seat.

The church service began with prayer and singing. Finally, the offering was completed, there was a baptism of a small child, and the minister gave his lengthy sermon. The sermon seemed as though it would never end. How the minister, Reverend Milo Koehn (pronounced Cane) could seem to say the same thing over and over again and hold everyone's attention amazed Adam. But all persons in the congregation remained still and seemed to hang onto every word. Reverend Koehn finally concluded his sermon, they sang one last song from the hymnal, and the service was over.

Finally, now that the service had concluded, Adam hoped that he would be able to see who the mysterious young woman was. He stood up and moved to another more advantageous position so he could get to a better viewing angle. There were so many people standing around in her same vicinity that he could not really see her. Finally, he moved down the center isle to a location that was nearer to hers. He moved precisely into her visual field and was startled to see Sarah. How did she come to be here? What had happened that she was here with her parents? What had occurred that she was apparently accepted back into her family? Adam was suddenly filled with questions for which he had no answers.

Sarah was there with her mother and father. Adam tried his very best to move closer to her to say 'Hello'. But there were so many people talking to her and her parents that he was not allowed to move closer. He tried desperately to get closer to Sarah so he could say something to her. Now, they were moving out into the side isle and beginning to walk toward the back of the sanctuary near the main doors. They were slowly moving out of the church. He simply had to move to their location to say something to her before they left. But how? Everyone was moving together, and he couldn't break into that crowd.

As Sarah and her parents walked out of the main doors at the rear of the sanctuary, Adam rushed through the doors just ahead of them.

Adam was finally able to force himself through the throng of people and then stopped directly in front of Sarah. Even though he was out of breath, he said "Hello Sarah. How have you been?"

He didn't know what else to say. He wanted to say, "I love you, Sarah. I have longed to be near you!" But, of course he didn't. After all, she was married. He looked at her and saw that she was even more beautiful than he recalled. The past two years had apparently been kind to her.

Sarah seemed to be unaware that Adam had approached her. When she saw him, she looked down and then slowly looked up into his eyes. Her face began to flush, her cheeks turning pinkish red. Not knowing quite what to say, she quietly said, "Hello Adam. And…how have you been? You have grown—I mean, you look very mature," she said quietly.

She looked down again as Adam hurriedly spoke, his words pouring out… "Can we talk sometime? Are you here for a visit? Is your husband Richie here?" His questioned flowed like water.

Sarah replied, "Yes—we can talk sometime. I…I would like that," she continued quietly. "It would be OK for you to call me at my parent's home. I'll be there."

Adam was pleased but confused. He thought, *Why would it be OK to call her at her parents' home? Would her husband not be there? She is married, so why would it be OK for me to call her to set a time to talk?* He had many questions at that moment that needed to be answered. But now was not the time or the place for them to be asked.

Chapter 21

As Adam and his mother and father drove home in the horse-drawn buggy, he remained rather quiet for the duration of the five-mile ride. His mother and father talked while Adam drove Ginger home. The staccato of the Ginger's hooves striking the hard packed road, and the drone of the voices of his mother and father through the noise of wind whistling around the buggy canopy lulled his mind nearly into a state of sleep. But rather than sleeping, he was thinking—thinking about Sarah, seeing her again so suddenly, so unexpectedly. Why was she there? Where was Richie her husband? Why was she with her parents at church when she had essentially been excommunicated from the Aldeman Mennonite Order and banned from her family?

This was all very confusing. Something had happened in Sarah's life, and he intended to find out what it was. He wondered how long he should wait before calling her. She said it would be OK to call. He didn't know how long she would be at her parent's home, so he felt he should call soon, or he might miss her. She would probably be going back to where she is living with her husband.

But still again he wondered, why was she here with her family when she had essentially been excommunicated from both her family and their church? Then, why was she with her parents, and importantly, why was she with them at church that day? Why were people trying to talk with her? Again, something has happened, and it must be important.

Adam decided to call her that evening. Since his family had a telephone installed in their home, he felt that he had the freedom to use it. But he would have to ask his mother or father to remind him of the telephone number for the Goering household, in other words, Sarah's parents. And, of course Adam's parents will be curious as to why he would ask for it. He would have to explain that he saw Sarah at church that day and she had said that it was OK for him to call her.

And, they would wonder why she had said that it was OK for him to call her, particularly since she was married. And they will also wonder why she was with her parent's at church when she had been excommunicated from her family. And further, they would wonder why she was there in the first place since she had been excommunicated from the Wheatland Mennonite Church because she had married a man who was 'of the world'. He would have to explain that he had no answers to their questions and would tell them what he learned after he had met with her.

Something strange had happened in Sarah's life, and Adam was anxious to know what it was. So, he had decided to call her that evening. Since he had not called their home for over nearly two years, he had to ask his parents to remind him of the telephone number for the Goering home. And, as he expected, they asked the questions he had predicted they would ask—the whys…and on and on. He would explain that he did not know the answers to those questions, but since Sarah had said that it was alright to call her at her parent's home, he needed their telephone number, and maybe when he talked with her, he would have some answers. They gave him the number. He then hesitated, took a deep breath and called the Goering home and asked for Sarah.

After answering his telephone call, and acknowledging Adam who had called, Sarah's mother asked with an unusually stern sound in her voice, "Did Sarah say that it was alright to call her?" she asked.

Adam responded that when they talked at church that morning, Sarah had said that he could call, and that she would like it if he would.

Her mother said, "Very well then, I will call her to the phone." She sounded rather strange, as though she was hesitant to allow Adam to talk to her daughter.

Adam waited nervously for Sarah to say 'Hello'. Time passed, and she still had not come to the telephone. How long should he wait, he wondered. Perhaps she had decided not to talk to him after all. He wondered if he should continue waiting. Another five minutes passed, and Adam was about to hang up, when Sarah said, "Hello Adam?"

The phone had been moved away from Adam's ear since he was about to hang up, but he faintly heard Sarah's voice.

"Hello Sarah? Are you there?" Adam spoke as he quickly placed the telephone receiver back to his ear.

"I said 'hello' to you, Adam," Sarah replied, "but it didn't sound like anyone was there. I'm sorry it took me so long to come to the telephone. I was almost too slow making up my mind about talking with you. But, on the other hand,

I wanted to talk to you. I'm sorry I was so slow in reaching a decision."

Adam replied, "I thought that maybe you weren't coming to the phone, so I was about to hang up, and then call back. But then I faintly heard your voice and quickly put the phone back near my ear. I was hoping that it wasn't my imagination. I'm glad it was you!"

"I think it would be good if we met somewhere so we can talk, Adam. I don't know where that would be, but it needs to be some place where we would be alone so I can tell you all that has happened," Sarah said with a degree of certainty in her voice. If her voice was any indication, she sounded as though she had matured a great deal during the past two years.

"I have thought about you a lot over the past two years Sarah—wondering how you were doing and wondering where you were. I met with your mother at one time, but she didn't have much information to share about your whereabouts," Adam quickly shared.

He was afraid that if he said too much, Sarah would decide that she didn't want to talk with him, and he would lose contact with her again. So, he decided not to say anything more. He would let Sarah talk, and perhaps they could meet somewhere so that could share their experiences over the past two years.

"Do you have any suggestions regarding where we can get together, Adam?" Sarah asked. "It would need to be a place where would be alone. I just don't know where that would be."

Adam thought for a moment, and then replied, "We could talk in my car. I have one now. Or, we could go someplace to have some ice cream or something—you know, a restaurant. If we went to Wheatland, Kansas they have two restaurants. We could check them out and find one that doesn't have a lot of people in it. How about that possibility?"

"I would rather it be where the people don't know me. I feel rather strange when I am out and about where people from our community can see me. Since I left our community in somewhat of a hurry two years ago, and since I disappointed my family and our church, and was essentially excommunicated from both, I felt like I was a sinner or something—like I don't belong in our community anymore. I wouldn't want people staring at me and wondering why I am here, and I wouldn't want to give you a reputation of being with a woman who has been excommunicated from our church—a 'fallen woman', so to speak."

Sarah continued as though she was ready to talk, "At church when you saw me, I was being treated by the other members as somewhat of a stranger. They wondered why I was there since I had been excommunicated from the Alderman Mennonite Order after marrying a man 'of the world'. My parents helped me by simply saying, and without explaining, that it was OK, that I had been accepted back into our family as their daughter."

Adam then suggested that they drive to another town, one where they may not be known. Conway, Kansas wasn't too far away, but it was out of their county, and people there probably wouldn't know them.

"How about that, Sarah?" Adam asked.

"OK," Sarah replied. "That sounds like a good place. Would tomorrow evening be good for you Adam?"

"Sure. What do you mean by evening?" Adam asked. "Do you mean evening-evening like 6:00 pm at supper time, or 8:00 pm like later in the evening?"

"How about splitting the difference and make it 7:00 pm so the supper crowd probably won't still be there, and we will be more apt to be alone, or at least nearly so."

"Sounds good to me," Adam responded. "I'll drive to your place to pick you up if that is OK. Will your husband be there? I worry about him since he would be wondering why you and I would be going someplace alone together. That wouldn't seem right since you are a married woman."

"That is one of the things I want you to know about me, Adam. Some things have changed in my life," Sarah replied.

That was all that she said. After that brief statement, she was silent. Adam didn't know what to say, and quickly decided not to pursue the topic unless she brought it up again. Now, he was really confused. What did she mean?

He thought it best to continue without asking, "I'll see you tomorrow evening at 7:00 pm, Sarah," Adam said at the conclusion of their conversation. "That will put us in Conway, Kansas at about 7:30 pm. Is that OK?"

"That sounds good, Adam," Sarah replied. "I'll see you then."

Chapter 22

Adam slowly placed the receiver back on the telephone. His thoughts were turning quickly into questions. Why was she here? Why had she been reunited with her family who had excommunicated her, and apparently united with their Mennonite Order and their church? Why was she so mysterious? Why did she say, "Some things have changed in my life?" Apparently, her husband was not with her. But why? Of course, he could not have been here with Sarah since after he married her, he was not allowed in her family's home. Something had, indeed, changed in Sarah's life. But what was it? He hoped that these questions would be answered tomorrow evening. It was going to be hard to wait that long to find out what Sarah was going to say. But, of course, he must.

He went to bed early that night, hoping that morning would come sooner that way. He had an entire day of farm work waiting for him the next day besides his morning and evening chores. But of course that would help the time to pass more quickly. Then would come dinner, and patiently waiting for 6:45 pm when he would get into his 1950 Dodge sedan and drive to the Goering farm to meet Sarah for their time alone.

He had waited, or at least hoped, for the time when he and Sarah would be together again, and now that desire would be satisfied. At least, if nothing else, they would be together to talk. He would then hopefully find answers to the many questions he had held with him over the past two years.

It was difficult to think about anything else while he drifted off to sleep the night before he was to see Sarah again. And she was on his mind when he awakened the next morning. He completed his morning chores without really thinking about them. He rechecked what he had accomplished and was satisfied that everything had been completed well. He then went to the house and ate the good breakfast that his mother had carefully prepared for him, although when he finished, he could hardly remember eating.

He had no idea what he would learn that evening. It may be nothing more than to tell him that she was happily married. He had heard nothing by way of the Wheatland Mennonite Church grape vein. If something dramatic happened in the life of a member of their congregation, the word would frequently spread throughout the community with uncanny speed.

His mother recognized his distant look while he ate, and she asked, "Are you all right, Adam? I have never known you to be so quiet. Is something wrong?"

Adam replied, "No…there is nothing wrong, and I feel OK. I guess I'm just sort of tired. I am to see Sarah tonight. I'm going over to the Goering house to see her. We'll go to a restaurant or somewhere else like that so we can talk— somewhere where no one knows us. I'm just wondering whether something has happened in her life. But I guess I'll find out tonight."

"What about her husband?" Adam's mother asked. "Won't he wonder why you are going out with Sarah?"

"That's what I don't understand, mother. She doesn't seem to be concerned about that. And beyond that, he doesn't even appear to be here with her. That's what I'm wondering about. Sarah was banned from her home, but now she is back apparently in good stead with her parents. She was banned from our church and our Aldeman Mennonite Order, but she was in church yesterday. Something has changed in her life and her relationship with her parents and our church. That's what I want to find out."

Adam put his all into the work that was assigned to him that day. His father had planned for him to begin plowing a relatively small forty-acre piece of land west of their house where he planned to plant cane sorghum that would grow and eventually be ground into ensilage. It would then be blown into one of their three silos for winter feed for their cattle. In those sixty-foot high silos, the sorghum would ferment and be ready to feed their dairy cattle and Adam's beef cattle during the winter. Forty acres of thickly growing cane sorghum would provide plenty of nutritious forage for the cattle during the upcoming winter. Since cane sorghum is very much like sugar cane, it ferments nicely, and becomes highly nutritious feed for cattle.

When 6:00 pm came around, Adam drove the tractor and plow back into the farm yard and asked his father whether he could come in and clean up and be ready for supper so he could leave their farm by around 6:45 pm to drive to the Goering farm to pick up Sarah for their evening of becoming reacquainted and talking. His father agreed that this was an important evening, and it was OK to stop the field work early.

Adam had a strange feeling that he would be somewhat uncomfortable driving over to see Sarah, her being married and all. But, after all, maybe his being there could be justified since they had been friends throughout their school days and beyond. On the other hand, Adam had had such strong feelings for her, and was extremely jealous of Richie who had in essence taken Sarah away from him. Those feelings of jealousy had remained with him since the time Sarah left with him.

So, maybe he shouldn't be going over to see Sarah at all. Deep inside of him he had a growing feeling that it may be pointless. After all, she was a married woman. And it seemed nearly sinful that they would be together even just for talking. He still had strong feelings for Sarah—feelings that he felt were those of love. So, with those feelings that he had for her, perhaps their being together to just talk might be a sin in the eyes of the Alderman Mennonite Order and his family.

Even in light of those mixed feelings, Adam bathed, ate a hurried supper, brushed his teeth, combed his hair and changed into nicer clothes than those he typically wore around the house. He didn't want to wear his best clothes, but he wanted to look presentable. He wanted to impress Sarah, but not appear as though he was going to a dress-up affair. He wanted what he was wearing to be subtle but nice and as stylish as their conservative Order would allow. Most of all, he wanted his evening with Sarah to be direct in regard to finding out why she had essentially run away with

Richie two years ago and married him, why she was here now, and what had apparently happened in her life that resulted in all of the changes that had recently occurred, those being her relationship with her family, their church, and the Aldeman Mennonite Order.

At 6:45 pm, Adam jumped into his plain old Dodge car and was ready to drive to the Yoder farm when he noticed that the gas gauge in his car indicated that he probably would not have enough fuel to drive the 25 miles to Conway, Kansas and back without worrying about running out of gas. So, he hurriedly drove to their large storage building that was used to house farm equipment and to the overhead gas tank that stood next to it. He jumped out of his car, removed the gas cap and filled the gas tank with fuel. It was now almost 5 minutes till seven o'clock, so he was going to be late.

Adam jumped back into his car, and quickly drove down their long driveway onto the main road. He drove as fast as he safely could on a sand and gravel covered road that could cause a car that is driven too fast to slide from side to side. He arrived at the Yoder farm at exactly 5 minutes after 7:00 pm, so at this point he was only five minutes late.

He sat in his car for a moment, still hesitant to be alone with Sarah. But his curiosity was stronger than his hesitancy to be with her, and so he left his car and walked up to the Goering farm house and knocked on the door that he knew led to the kitchen.

Sarah's mother came to the door and asked Adam to come inside, which he did. She told Adam that Sarah would be with him in a moment and offered him a chair in the living room. After he waited patiently for a few moments, Sarah came down the stairway and greeted him. "Hello Adam. It's good to see you again. Are you ready to go?"

Adam stood looking at Sarah. As he had noticed when he saw her at church, she was even more beautiful than he remembered. Again, he thought that marriage and the last two years had been good to her. Her blond hair was fixed neatly into a bow inside of her white cap, and he noticed that her shapely figure could not be hidden beneath the conservative plain long dress that she was wearing. She was, indeed, a beautiful young woman.

"Well, are you ready to go?" Sarah asked again. Adam had been standing and staring at her for longer than he realized.

Sarah's question brought him out of his daze, and he responded, "Oh…I'm sorry, Sarah. Yes, I'm ready. Let's go!" Adam replied.

She said goodbye to her mother, and they both exited the Goering house and walked to Adam's very plain car. He was only slightly embarrassed that it wasn't a sleek car 'of the world' like Richie had. But Adam also knew that Richie evidently wasn't there.

He opened the door on the passenger side for Sarah. She seated herself, and Adam walked quickly over to the driver's side and closed the door.

Adam turned to her, "I apologize for such a plain car, Sarah. I am sure that you and your husband have a much nicer one, one that is designed for 'the world' that you live in now."

Sarah did not respond. But instead, she was quietly looking down at the floor of the car. She then plaintively looked out of the window on her side. She began, "We'll talk when we arrive at the restaurant, Adam. I don't want to talk now." Then, she was quiet, unusually quiet.

Rather than try to begin a conversation, Adam started his car, turned it around in the large open area in front of the Goering house and outbuildings, and drove down the driveway onto the main road toward the highway that was three miles south of the Goering farm. From there, they would head west toward Conway, a relatively short 25 miles away.

Their drive along the highway was filled with silence. Sarah sat quietly looking out of the window on her side of the car, while Adam drove safely and slowly as he always did. Driving a car at 50 miles per hour seemed extremely fast in comparison to the Sunday drive in the horse-drawn buggy with his parents. He didn't drive a car often since on the farm he most frequently drove their tractor or the old pickup truck. But he was a good driver, and Sarah felt that she was safe with him, much safer than with Richie who liked to drive fast and show off the car he was driving.

Adam was anxiously awaiting the talk that he and Sarah was to have when they finally arrived at a restaurant where they hoped they would be quietly alone. He had no idea which restaurant that might be, but he was fairly sure that he would find a suitable one for their conversation.

As his mind wandered, he was beginning to reconsider why they had to drive so far to simply talk. But, remembering 'why' resumed its place in his mind. It would simply be best to be in a distant community since something had apparently happened in Sarah's life, a change that had brought her back to her home and seemed to have reinstated her membership in her family unit and their church. But, still, according to many people in their community, she was married. So, to observe Adam and Sarah together in the same restaurant and in the same booth within their own community could very well be taken as scandalous, to say the least.

Chapter 23

The tiny town of Conway, Kansas was eventually seen on the horizon. It was rather dark, but the lights that alerted them that they were nearing the outskirts of that community were coming into view. Conway, Kansas was a small community in the central part of the state of Kansas, but it was considered by the Aldeman Mennonite community to be 'of the world'. Therefore, it was apt to have a few more restaurants and stores that would cater to that population of the state.

As they drove into town from the east side, all they saw were nice relatively small houses with neat yards that came into view as they passed down what appeared to be the main street. The street was a rough one but it was paved. The town fathers didn't seem to take care of the bumps Adam and Sarah were experiencing as they drove further into town.

Eventually they left what appeared to be the residential area and began to see some businesses lining the street. No restaurants came into view as they moved further west through the small town. They continued in a straight line through what appeared to be the main part of the business district and began to move on out of that section into the western area of town. Filling stations came into view, along with two automobile dealerships. As they passed the car dealerships, they found themselves next to the parking lot of a truck stop. The neon sign said, 'Roadway Café and Truck Stop'. That was just what Adam was looking for! He supposed that there would be no one from the Wheatland, Kansas community there who would recognize them.

Adam pulled slowly into the large parking lot where several eighteen wheeler trucks were sitting near the fuel pumps. He then counted five cars parked near the restaurant. He drove up to the restaurant and parked near what appeared to be the main door. The restaurant within the truck stop appeared rather small, but it seemed to be a perfect place for their conversation.

He got out of his side of the car and walked around to open the opposite door for Sarah. She seemed somewhat surprised that Adam was so courteous, but she stepped from the car while Adam locked it and they both walked toward the door of the restaurant. He opened the restaurant door for Sarah as she entered.

"Thank you Adam. I'm not used to a man opening doors for me, but thank you very much!" Sarah remarked.

Adam didn't respond, he just smiled and continued to walk into the restaurant to locate a booth where they could talk without disturbance. At the moment only one seemed to be available, so he looked at Sarah in an inquiring way to silently confirm as to whether the booth that was available was OK. She nodded affirmatively, and so they walked to it and sat down, Adam on one side of the table, and Sarah on the other. He didn't want to be seen sitting on the same side of the booth as Sarah just in case someone who knew them happened to enter the restaurant.

They sat quietly, neither knowing quite how to begin a conversation. Momentarily, a server came to their booth to see what they wanted to order. Adam looked at Sarah in an affirmative manner, indicating that she could order whatever she wanted.

Sarah looked inquiringly at Adam, "What are you having?"

Adam told the server, "I'll just have a Pepsi Cola."

"I'll have the same," Sarah replied.

A cold carbonated soda was often considered by their Old Order Mennonite customs to be 'of the world' and should be avoided. But, since they were both out of their community, and in a restaurant to talk for a while, Adam felt free to order something that he ordinarily would not have if he were back home. Sarah felt that since Adam had ordered something out of the ordinary, she might as well too. They didn't feel as though they were committing a sin.

The server left, and both Sarah and Adam remained silent for a few moments until it began to become uncomfortable for both of them.

So, Adam, leaning forward slightly said, "It was good to see you at church, Sarah. For a while, I wasn't sure it was you. I thought perhaps it was someone who resembled you. You look different. I mean…but, not in a bad way. I mean you look…" trying to search for words. "I mean, you look good…just a little more mature, not like the last time I saw you. I mean that you do look good…I mean I like the way you look…I'm not saying this very well, am I?"

He finally said, "I'm sorry that I didn't say what I wanted to say. I meant to say that you look absolutely beautiful, Sarah." Then he looked down and remained quiet.

Adam was having a hard time finding words to express his thoughts. He felt very nervous. He never in his entire life thought that he would be sitting across a restaurant with Sarah. He had been so sure that she was completely out of his life, gone forever. But here she was sitting across from him. It seemed almost as though a miracle had occurred. But, why? Why was she here?

He still had no idea why she was here—apparently without her husband, and apparently welcomed back into her family. What's wrong? Why doesn't she talk?

Finally, Sarah began. She smiled, and said in all seriousness, "You're probably wondering why I called this meeting," and then smiled mischievously, expecting Adam to get the joke and laugh.

Rather than laughing, he looked at her strangely and simply said, "What?"

"Oh Adam, I was just kidding. I thought you would find the humor in what I said. I have been waiting and expected you to begin a conversation of some kind so we could talk, but you've been very quiet. So, I figured that I would get it started somehow, and that was the only way that came to mind."

Adam replied, "I guess I've been quiet because I really didn't know what to say, Sarah. I have wondered why you are here. Why you seem to have been welcomed back into your family and our church. I have wondered why you are here without your husband. I have so many questions that I haven't known where to begin a conversation. I have thought about you so often over the past two years, but never thought I would see you again. And there you were at church. I was almost dumbfounded with surprise. It was wonderful to see you again."

He continued, "Can you answer any of my questions? I have been so curious since I saw you in church that I really haven't thought about much else. I mean, I don't want to pry into your life, but I'd like so much to hear answers to some of my questions. Can you do that? Or, I guess I should say, would you feel comfortable answering my questions?"

Sarah was quiet again. She looked down at the table as tears filled her eyes. "Oh Adam…I…don't know where to…"

The server came to their table just as Sarah was beginning to say something that seemed important. The server sat the soft drinks on their table and asked if they would like anything else. Adam looked at Sarah who shook her head to indicate that she did not want anything else, as did Adam. So, the server left and went to another table.

Adam looked again at Sarah and said, "You were beginning to say…?"

Sarah began again, "I wish that I didn't feel compelled to tell you, Adam, but I feel that it is best that I do."

She paused, took a deep breath, and then said, "Richie left me. He has been gone for nearly a year now. He always seemed unhappy when we were together. He didn't want a home and a family. He told me that so many times after we had become married. He hurt me deeply when he would say those things. It was as though his intent was to make me unhappy."

"He was nearly always gone until late at night. I continued to wonder if there was someone else who he was seeing. I tried not to think about that possibility, but the evidence was there—just little bits of traces of evidence that he was seeing someone else."

"We were never together intimately. He didn't seem to desire to be with me in that way. It appeared that he had conquered what he thought would be impossible, that is to run away and marry someone who was not supposed to marry outside of her conservative Order of Mennonite. And, after he had completed his conquest, he seemed to not want me anymore."

"He left about a year ago. I thought that he might return, but he has not. It has been long enough. In my mind, he is gone forever. I went to a judge at the courthouse where we were living in Clairmont, Nebraska to seek an annulment of our marriage. The judge was very kind and understanding, but also strict in abiding by the law. However, the annulment was finally granted two weeks ago."

"So, I returned to my home to ask for forgiveness, and reinstatement in my family and in our church. I have been forgiven by my family, and with their blessing and intervention, I have been received back into our Mennonite Order. I am so happy to be back with my family and our church. I feel so relieved and happy. It's hard to describe."

"But," Adam replied, "Are you not still married? If you are, we probably should not be together alone." He was not sure what an annulment of marriage consisted of and was unsure how to ask Sarah to explain.

Sarah replied quickly, "But, you are wrong, Adam. Not only was our marriage annulled which means that it no longer exists, and since Richie deserted me over a year ago, according to the doctrine of our Order of Mennonite, Richie is dead. After all the time he has been absent from me, he is considered dead. And since our marriage has been annulled, our marriage is dead. The annulment is final. I am no longer married, and in the eyes of our Mennonite doctrine, I am an unmarried maiden."

She continued as though she had been waiting for a long time to say all that she was saying. It was pouring forth as rainwater pours and it felt as though she couldn't stop until she had said everything that had been kept inside of her for many months.

"I don't know why I did such an unthinking thing in the first place. I think I was so taken by his shiny car, his air of independence, his smooth manner of talking to me…it was nearly as though I was hypnotized into doing something that I would never consider doing. It was though I fell into something that I will regret for the rest of my life."

"I ran away and married someone who I would never in my life have married, someone who I *never* should have been with in the first place. I have felt awful for so long. I have been so miserable, wondering about my family, my church, and of course you. I sinned in the eyes of my family and my church—in your eyes!"

Tears began to well up in Sarah's eyes, and they began to run down her now rosy cheeks. Jacob started to say something, then stopped. And, then he began again.

"Sarah, I have thought about you so much over the past two years. When I would begin to fall asleep at night, my thoughts would most likely turn to you—wondering where you were, how you were, if you ever thought of me. I tried not to think of you. But you were always there in my thoughts. I truly felt as though I had been cheated out of my dream of being with you. When I thought of my future, it always had *you* and only you as an important part. But then I would remember that you were married, and I knew that my thoughts and dreams of our future would never happen."

He began again, "And, I want you to know that in my eyes, you did not sin. You were infatuated with something that I could not offer. You were young and impressed with all that Richie had. And you did something that just wasn't you. You ran away and married someone you would otherwise have never thought of marrying. And it didn't work, and now you are back home, and we are together talking alone, just like I have dreamed of over the past two years. Oh, I have loved you from afar, Sarah, more than I ever thought that I could love someone!"

Adam looked down at the table, and in a quiet voice said, "And, I am sure that I have said much more than I should have. And I'm sorry if I have made you feel uncomfortable."

"No, Adam, you have not. I truly feel comfortable with you. And, your words are ones that I love to hear. I'm just so confused right now. I waited for nearly a year to hear from the man who I married. I waited and heard nothing. I don't know if he is dead or alive. I do know that he is still married unless he somehow had it annulled. But I am sure that I would have somehow been notified if he tried to do that. So, if he is still married, I am assured that I am not. As I said, in the eyes of our church and my family, Richie is dead. Our marriage is dead."

"But," she continued, "I feel like a wandering soul—a person who has been displaced. I am back home, but I do not feel as though I belong since it has been so long. I love my parents. I have tried to locate my friends who I grew up with but have had a difficult time doing that. Most of them are married or have otherwise moved away from our community. I'm not sure if I belong here. But I am thankful that our church has accepted my return and I am reinstated within the Aldeman Mennonite Order. I wasn't sure if I would be, but I am thankful that I am."

"I have thought about you, Adam. You have had a special place in my mind and my heart over the past two years. I had feelings for you when we were in grade school and after we graduated. I thought that they were the same feelings that you said you had for me. But, as time passed, I became so mixed up. I could see my future only as one working in a house—a house wife doing housework, raising chickens, having babies and caring for them—just the typical house and wifely duties of a Mennonite woman living on a farm. I felt that I needed more than that, that I needed to be productive in other ways. The problem has been, however, I haven't been able to determine what those 'other ways' are. I suppose that I need help. I need help to assist me in understanding myself. What am I supposed to be, what am I supposed to do when I grow up?"

With that last statement, Sarah looked at Adam and smiled her mischievous smile, thinking that Adam would get the humor of that last phrase. When he didn't seem to get the humor, she said it again, "What am I supposed to be when I grow up? Do you get the humor in that, Adam? You could at least smile if you do." Sarah smiled again, and Adam finally joined in the bit of humor that Sarah had interjected into the conversation.

Adam wasn't thinking of actual 'humor' when Sarah introduced her bit of satire into their conversation. He was actually thinking of what Sarah *could* do. She could marry him. She could become his wife! He could think of nothing better than being with her for the rest of his life—to have and to hold from that day forth—as they said in marriage ceremonies.

He looked down at the table where they sat and smiled just a little at Sarah's attempt to interject a small amount of humor into their conversation. He had so much he wanted to say to her, but he didn't want to make her feel uncomfortable being with him. He wanted her to know how much he cared for her, how much he felt that he loved her. But he held that part of the conversation back. He felt that perhaps he had already said too much. Maybe some other time when they had spent more time together, but probably not the first time he had seen her in two years, and not at this time in her life.

They both remained quiet for a moment. It was now 9:30 pm and the drive back to their homes took at least 30 or more minutes. Adam did not want the evening to end. He had waited more than two years to see Sarah again, and the evening had passed by so quickly that he was afraid that perhaps Sarah was still somewhat confused—that perhaps she would decide that she didn't want to see him again. But he also didn't want to outlive his welcome.

Sarah had been open in her conversation with him, and she seemed as though she enjoyed being with him again after two years, particularly since so many things had happened in her young life. Adam simply felt that it was time to conclude their evening. Perhaps if he didn't outlive his welcome, Sarah might be happier to see him if they were together again.

Adam suggested that he drive her back to her house. She looked down and nodded her head. She didn't say anything. She simply nodded in agreement. He couldn't tell if she was sad, or in agreement since she was so silent. They both rose from their booth and exited the restaurant after Adam paid for their sodas and left a small tip for the waitress—15% of $2.50 wasn't very much. He felt rather guilty since he had spent such a small amount of money compared to all the time that they had spent in the restaurant that evening.

Chapter 24

The drive back to Sarah's home was quiet. She did say that it was a nice evening. The weather was good, and the ride was a pleasant one. Other than that, she didn't utter a word. Adam was afraid that he had perhaps said something during the evening that had made her uncomfortable. Perhaps she was wishing that she hadn't accepted his invitation to join him for the evening. He didn't know why she was so quiet.

Adam pulled into the long driveway of the Goering farm and pulled his car to a stop near the back door to their house. He shut the engine off and started to tell Sarah that he had enjoyed being with her. Before he could say anything, Sarah began to talk.

"Adam," she began, "I want you to know that I enjoyed being with you this evening. At the beginning of the evening, I felt somewhat awkward since we hadn't talked or really been together for such a long time. Somehow, I feel like I am still married, but I keep telling myself that I am not. Our marriage has been terminated—annulled. I've got to keep telling myself that. I do want to be with you again, Adam. I really do. As I said earlier, I am confused right now. I don't know what to do with my life. I feel empty—alone. Of course, I've been alone most the time since I became married. I simply never saw Richie. He removed himself from my life right after we became married. Even though we were never intimate, he had accomplished what he had intended, and then he left!"

Adam was silent for a few moments, and then replied, "I've never been married, so I don't know what it feels like to have it annulled. I wish I could make your life full again, Sarah. I wish that I could fill the emptiness that you feel. I wish so many things right now, but most of all I want you to be happy. I want you to feel fulfilled. I don't want you to feel empty and alone."

"Oh Adam," Sarah said in response, "I feel good being with you. I feel happier than I have felt in a long, long time. I want to be with you again when you have the time."

When she had expressed her feelings, she leaned over to Adam and gave him a kiss. Adam, feeling rather startled put his arms around her and pulled her close to him. She didn't resist but moved closer. He held her close to him for what seemed like a long time. Her arms then reached out and held Adam in return. They remained in their embrace, clinging to each other, not wanting to let go. Adam felt tears dropping on his sleeve and he realized that Sarah was crying, he felt her sobs against his chest.

Suddenly, Sarah pulled away from Adam, "Oh Adam, I am so sorry. I didn't mean to cry. But it was such a relief to be held. I felt as though the frustrations and anger I have felt for the past two years were lifted from me for a moment. Oh, thank you, Adam! Please, just hold me."

Adam put his arms around Sarah again, as she put her arms around him in return. They remained like that for what seemed to be a long time. To Adam, it was a dream come true. He had wanted to hold Sarah close to him since they were in the eighth grade. Now, they were both twenty-two years of age, and he was finally given the opportunity to put his arms around the young woman who he had loved from afar for so many years.

Suddenly, once again, Sarah pulled away from the embrace. "Thank you for holding me, Adam. I felt so comfortable in your arms that I'm afraid that I got carried away. I hope that I didn't embarrass you."

"You didn't embarrass me. In fact, I was about to thank you for allowing me the opportunity to hold you close to me. I have wanted to do that for such a long time. To me, it was wonderful to be so close to you. I have dreamed of that for such a long time. Thank you—thank you, Sarah! I love you so much. I have dreamed of this moment so often, but never thought my dream would come true."

"Oh Adam, I think that I embarrassed myself. But, as I said, for that brief moment I felt as though a terrible weight had been lifted from me—a weight that I have been living with for the past two years. But I think that I should be going into the house now. My mother and father will be wondering what happened to me."

"Yes, I suppose so," Adam replied. "I really don't want this evening to end. But, if we can be together again, I can look forward to that. You did say that you wanted to be with me again, didn't you?"

Sarah smiled and nodded affirmatively. "Yes, Adam, I do. I want to be with you again sometime soon. I was happier this evening than I have been for a very long time. And I want to be happy again."

"I'll do my best to make you happy," Adam replied. "I, more than anything else want to make you happy—and I hope for a very long time."

"Oh Adam, I have longed to hear those words. I feel so undeserving of your feelings for me. I really do. I feel as though I deserted you, my family, my church, everyone who mattered to me. And, now that I am with you again, I feel as though I can feel happy again. But I want you to be happy too."

"Oh I am, Sarah. I am truly happy just being with you again."

Adam walked Sarah to the door of the Goering house. They stood at the back door momentarily holding hands. As they held hands, they looked into each other's eyes just as they did in the eighth grade at Fairmont Rural School. Both were silent while Sarah looked longingly at Adam. He wanted desperately to kiss her, but he resisted his desire and said "Good night. I will call you so we can be together again soon."

"Oh please do, Adam," Sarah said quiet, still looking into Adam's eyes.

With that, Adam walked slowly back to his car, sat for a moment trying to recount all that happened during the evening with Sarah, and then started the car and drove down the long driveway onto the main road to drive back to their farm.

At the moment, Adam's thoughts were spinning around and around. What had happened during that evening? Adam couldn't recall everything, but what he did remember was a blur of emotion between Sarah and himself. As he sat behind the steering wheel of his car, his heart was beating rapidly, he felt light and airy. What had happened to bring forth the feelings for him that Sarah had expressed toward the end of their evening together? All that he knew at that moment in time was that he was extremely happy—joyous, in fact! All that he had dreamed of over the past six-plus years seemed to be becoming a reality.

He drove back to their farm, parked his car in the shed where other pieces of farm equipment were stored, and walked to the house. It was now nearly midnight, but he didn't feel tired. He climbed the stairs to his bedroom, began to undress and get ready for bed. But he still wasn't tired. He was so elated—his spirits were lifted so high that he didn't feel as though he would be able to sleep. He sat on the edge of his bed and recalled the softness of Sarah as he held her close to him, and as she enfolded him in her arms in return. He didn't want that feeling of Sarah's closeness to end, but of course it must, at least for tonight. He knew above all else that he wanted to be with Sarah again—very soon. And, when she had said that she wanted to be with him again, it seemed to be another dream come true.

At 1:00 am, he knew that he had to go to bed. He finished undressing, put on his pajamas, climbed down the thirteen steps to the downstairs bathroom to brush his teeth, climbed back up to his room, set his alarm for 6:00 am, and crawled into bed. As he pulled the blankets over him and nestled into the soft mattress, his eye lids became heavier. The next thing he knew, his alarm clock was chirping loudly, his hand hit the 'off' button, and he slowly emerged from the warmth of his bed. As his feet hit the cool, almost cold hardwood floor that always wakened him, he padded across the floor of his second story bedroom and once again began the trip down to the bathroom that had been designated as his to use to wash up, shave, take a brief shower, and be ready for another day of hard work on their large farm.

As Adam looked into the mirror at his half-grown beard, he noticed that his hair was nearly standing on end. How could any young woman consider what he saw in the mirror to be someone who was desirable to be with? But, as he combed his hair, shaved the areas where he did not want a beard to grow, that is everything on his face except around his chin, he began to notice that perhaps he wasn't such a bad looking guy after all.

He still felt light and airy from the night before. He had no idea that Sarah might want to be with him again. And their closeness at the end of their evening as they sat in his car was much beyond his wildest dreams. He had dreamed of holding her close to him, and of her enfolding him into her arms. Over the past two years he had dreamed of that but felt that it would probably never become a reality. But was it a dream? Was it truly real? It seemed that after all those years of dreaming, perhaps it *had* finally become a reality.

Now, he had to plan to see Sarah again, but he didn't want to call too soon to ask her out. She needed time to be alone with her family. Today was Tuesday. Perhaps it would be OK to see if she would be willing to be together on Saturday evening. So, he decided to call her that evening. He didn't want her to think that he was pressuring her to be with him. He realized that she needed time to heal.

Later that evening, at about 7:00 pm after he and his father and mother had finished eating supper, he supposed that the Goering's had probably finished theirs. So, he decided to call Sarah to see if she wanted to go out to have a soda or some ice cream on Saturday evening. He was hesitant to call again so soon, but he felt that he would never know if she wanted to be with him again unless he asked her out. She could always say 'No', but he truly hoped that she wouldn't.

Adam called the Goering's telephone number at just a little after 7:00 pm. When her mother answered the phone, he asked for Sarah. Her mother, as usual, asked who was calling. Adam said that it was he who was trying to get ahold of Sarah to ask her something. Her mother told him that she was not in at the moment and wasn't quite sure when she would be home.

Adam wasn't sure what to say. He really wanted to know where she was. He didn't want to sound possessive, but his first thought was that maybe Richie had located Sarah and was with her. His heart sank at that possibility. It wasn't probable, but he was not sure if that possibility did not exist. However, he told her mother politely that he would call again on another day.

Chapter 25

Today was Thursday. He had waited an additional day before calling Sarah. He was sure that her mother had told her that he had called on Tuesday evening and may have wondered why he didn't try to get in touch on Wednesday evening. He purposely, and perhaps even selfishly, wanted to wait a day so that she would have the opportunity to wonder about that. He felt just a little devious in doing it but thought it would be best so that she wouldn't feel that he was too obviously anxious to see her again.

There was a full day of chores and field work waiting for him on that day. So, he decided to call again that evening after supper. He was questioning whether Saturday might be too soon to be together with Sarah again. But, to him, Saturday evening was the time for being with someone special. At least that was what he had been told. And he thought so too.

All he could do was call Sarah and ask her if she would be willing to be with him again. He was still somewhat concerned that perhaps the reason Sarah had not been at home on Tuesday evening was that Richie had returned. Yet that didn't seem possible. However, his own insecurities were taking hold as they usually did when something good was beginning to take place in his life. He would find out when he called that evening.

So, later that day after he had finished his work in the fields that his father had planned for him, had completed his evening chores of feeding the livestock, and supper had been eaten, he left the table and dialed the phone number for the Goering household. He wasn't sure what would occur during the phone call, but he thought that he would at least give it a try. After all, Sarah had said the last time they were together that she would like to be with him again.

He dialed the Goering's telephone number, and after three distant rings, Sarah's mother answered.

"Hi Mrs. Goering," Adam tried his best to use his happiest voice, "this is Adam Yoder again, and I'm wondering if Sarah is there, and if I may talk with her?"

"Yes, Adam," she responded, "I'll call her to the phone," seeming to be more willing to allow him to speak to Sarah than before. He hoped it was a good sign.

A few moments passed, and then Adam heard Sarah's sweet voice, "Hi Adam! I've been thinking about you, hoping you would call. How have you been since we were last together?"

"Mostly thinking of you, Sarah. It's only been four days since we were together, but it seems much longer. That's the reason I'm calling. I have a question for you. Do you think that we could be together this coming Saturday evening? I think it would be nice if we could."

"I do too," was Sarah's quick reply. "I think it would be splendid. Give me a time, and I'll be ready."

"How about 7:00 pm? That way I'll have time to clean up after a day in the fields. And, I have a few head of steers in my herd that I'm trying to get ready to sell. I'll tell you about that when we're together. I can pick you up at 7:00 pm. Let me know what you would like to do. I don't really think that we need to go out of town unless you feel that we should. We have a good M & W Root Beer and hamburger place in Wheatland now. They serve right at the car. They have a hamburger with barbeque sauce that I have been craving."

"That sounds good to me," Sarah replied. "I'll see you at 7:00 pm."

Adam hung the telephone receiver back on the phone, thinking happy thoughts about Sarah. She actually acted as though she would be looking forward to being with him. Adam was almost beyond happy! But it was now only Thursday evening. Saturday seemed a long way off.

As Sarah hung up the telephone receiver at her parent's house, she felt a sense of gladness that she would be seeing Adam again so soon. However, what she was going to say during that evening worried her a little. She felt that he would understand her hesitancy and concerns, but still she wasn't sure how he would respond.

When she was with him on Sunday evening, she felt free, she felt truly alive for the first time in several years. It was such a lovely feeling to be held by someone who seemed to care deeply for her, and then to enfold him in her arms in return. She felt loved when she was with Adam—she felt cared for. It was the first time she had felt that way with a man for what seemed to be a very long time. On the other hand, she was afraid—afraid of entering a relationship of any kind so soon. She felt vulnerable, confused, and afraid of what the future would hold for her if she entered a serious relationship and then married again.

But, as she thought of Adam, she recalled that he had actually waited for her for more than two years to see if a miracle might happen that would bring her back to him. She was loved by him and had been for a number of years even dating back to when they were in their country school together playing soft ball and singing in the school choir.

Why should she be afraid? She cared for Adam. But did she love him? She wasn't sure. She said that she did, but was it true? There were moments the last time they were together when she truly felt love—a feeling of love that was deep down inside of her. Or was it that she wanted to love and to be loved? Was it simply a need that she had that she desired be fulfilled?

Sarah guessed that perhaps her feelings of confusion, or caution, were all a part of being a woman who had been abandoned by the man she had foolishly married. He had simply left soon after their marriage. They never had an intimate moment together. He had apparently conquered the impossible and then left her. He had somehow convinced her to leave all that she knew, all that she had in her life, took her away, conquered the seeming impossible, convincing her to marry a man who she was not even supposed to be associating with, and then left her.

Even before he left, even during their simple courthouse marriage ceremony, she already had feelings of uncertainty and guilt regarding what she had done to her family by essentially deserting them, leaving her good standing within their Mennonite Order—her church, leaving Adam the one who seemed to care deeply for her, and all because she wanted to leave her life on the farm, follow a shallow dream, a silly infatuation over a flashy car, and then exchange all that she knew, all that she had in her life for a brainless adventure.

Why had she done such a foolish thing? She absolutely did not know. The amazing thing was that her family, her church, her Mennonite Order, and Adam had all welcomed her return—no anger, no 'I told you so', no punishment. They simply welcomed her return with open arms. The love for her that welcomed her back into their fold was such a wonderful blessing.

She had dreaded what would be waiting for her when she returned home. But her return was nothing like she had expected. She experienced love, caring and joy from everyone, and most of all from Adam—dear sweet Adam who she thought would have given up on her long ago. But he hadn't given up. And in a way, she was happier now than she thought she could ever be. She was happy that Adam had not given up on his dream of being with her. She longed for love and caring, and Adam seemed to have more than his share to give to her.

So, why did her feelings of confusion worry her? Maybe it would simply take a while to become used to being back home, and to being with Adam. He had matured over the past several years and seemed to be a somewhat different person. The boy who she had fallen for in the eighth grade had grown into manhood. In some ways, he was the same 15 year-old who sang with her in the Fairmont Rural School last day of school chorus and played the part of Johnny Appleseed in the school play on that same day. She was proud of him, had told him so, and had confided in him that she had the same feelings for him as those he said in confidence that he had for her. It was such a sweet and innocent time in their lives.

But the years passed after they had graduated from the eighth grade, and as she matured, she had begun to grow apart from the Old Order Mennonite way of life. She had begun to change. Sarah's feelings about herself, her life on the farm were still clouding her mind, resulting in a sense of rebellion against all that she had in Cloud County—her future, her life. Those were the feelings that pushed her toward Richie, the young man who seemed to hold the key to the adventure that she wanted, or at least something that was beyond her future as a wife and mother trapped on a farm of an Old Order Mennonite farmer.

But that dream had betrayed her! She had been deserted and left alone in a strange town. It was not the dream that she had imagined it would be. Her dream had become a nightmare. Returning home was a true homecoming, a real blessing to be with those who loved and cared for her. However, she did not want to do anything rash when it came to Adam. Adam's feelings for her had not changed. He loved her. He wanted to be with her. The fact that she had married in haste, and she in essence had deserted him did not seem to concern to him. At least he did not seem angry or resentful. He had simply waited and hoped and dreamed that she would return, with no assurance that it would ever happen.

She knew deep down that she should feel lucky that such a fine young man as Adam would welcome her with open arms, who would love and cherish her in spite of all that had happened. So, why did she feel so confused? Sarah, again, supposed that it would just take some time to adjust to being back home, being with family and friends, and being with Adam. She felt justified in taking her time. It was best to simply adjust to being back home. It would take time.

Chapter 26

It was now Saturday morning, and Adam went about completing his morning chores of feeding cattle and calves, making sure all had adequate water and feed for the day. Once again there was a full day of field work waiting for him. The acreage that his father had acquired when they moved to Cloud County, Kansas was almost more than the two of them could handle. It was fortunate that Adam's father had recently hired two hired hands to help out with the hard work that was waiting for them each summer. One of the men went by the name of Slim Swansen, and the other by the name of Elmer Mowly. They were both hard working men—Slim being the youngest and Elmer the eldest.

Each day when Elmer came to work on the Yoder farm, he usually had a short stub of cigar stuck in the corner of her mouth, clenched there by his teeth, and tobacco stains were typically seen seeping down toward his chin, and the pungent odor emanating from his well-worn overalls led one to believe that his bathing habits were few and far between. In spite of what most observers would see as unseemly, he was a hardworking and very pleasant older man who didn't seem to mind the heat or the sweat that came from working on that large farm.

Slim Swansen, which was his real name, was a natural for his name. He was as 'slim' as a rail, and on weekends he drove a race car that he had built from scratch. He was a very religious young man who taught Sunday School at the United Methodist Church in Wheatland, Kansas. He felt that God had blessed him by bringing him a job at a good Mennonite farm. He was a hard worker, and very dependable in the completion of the daily tasks that were assigned to him.

In addition to hiring men to help with the day-to-day labor on their many acres, Adam was also glad that his father had shunned the days when Old Order Mennonites generally used horse-drawn farm implements or small tractors and shunned the extravagant pieces of equipment that they felt were 'of the world'. Those workhorse teams and small tractors moved at only three miles per hour in the field since they were pulling heavy equipment that sometimes dug deeply into the ground such as plows, disks and 'crust busters' that tilled the soil, and simply could not move with the speed necessary for the efficiency needed for day-to-day work on large farms.

The plows and other pieces of equipment of some Old Order Mennonite farmers who used horses and small tractors involved equipment with old fashion iron wheels and hand operated levers rather than newer tractors that were bigger, more powerful. Even though the tractors such as those used on the Yoder farm were larger and more powerful, the 'tires' on those powerful tractors were made of steel with heavy lugs that dug into the soil for traction. Rubber tires were considered 'of the world', and so were avoided by conservative Mennonite farmers. However, those big tractors could pull large farm implements that worked with greater efficiency in the fields, using hydraulic systems that made lifting and turning the equipment they were pulling much quicker and safer. They could cover more farmland in less time, making use of time-saving/labor-saving equipment, and thus increasing the efficiency of person-power, accountability of time and effort, and, in turn, farm profits.

The day went by slowly. At lunchtime, Adam ate quickly wanting to return to the fields in order to complete the plowing that had waited for him that morning. He wanted to complete the field work by at least 5:00 pm so that he could put the tractor away, bathe, shave and be ready to drive over to the Goering house to pick up Sarah by a little before 7:00 pm. He was not only going to be very happy to see Sarah, but he was also looking forward to driving to town with Sarah to stop at the M & W Drive-In to have one of those barbeque flavored hamburgers he had heard so much about and a cold root beer. At that time of the day he was very hungry, not having eaten since lunch time.

At 5:00 pm, he had nearly completed plowing the field that was assigned to him that day. The furrows were perfectly done—smooth, straight and at a correct depth of about 8 inches. He estimated that he had only three more trips back and forth through the field, and the plowing of that field would be completed. Each length of the field that he traveled was three-quarters of a mile in length, and back and forth to make one complete round was one and one-half miles in length. So, the going was slow.

When the plowing was complete for that field and the ends were blocked and finished to his satisfaction, he raised the hydraulic lever to bring the plow that was firmly attached to the rear of the tractor up out of the ground, put the transmission of the tractor in the fast road gear and sped out of the field onto the main road that would take him back home—two miles away. There he would park the tractor in the large storage shed, confirm with his father that he had finished plowing the field that was assigned to him, and then run to the house to bathe, shave, eat a little supper, and then drive to the Goering house to pick up Sarah for their date. It was now 5:45 pm, and just enough time to complete everything.

Quitting time during the week was generally around 8:00 pm or so when the sun was nearing the horizon and twilight was just around the corner. However, Adam was thankful that his father allowed him the latitude of quitting field work early on that Saturday evening so he could see Sarah.

Chapter 27

As soon as Adam finished a light supper that his mother had prepared for him, he went back to his room on the second floor to look in the mirror that was attached to the dresser to make sure that he looked as presentable as he wanted to for Sarah. He then rushed down the 13 steps of the stairway to the downstairs bathroom to brush his teeth, make sure that his hair was combed to his satisfaction, washed his face one more time and added a little after shave lotion to make sure that he smelled fresh even though he had showered after coming in from the field. When that was completed to the degree possible, he was ready for a wonderful evening with Sarah. He had waited all week for this moment and was happy that it had finally arrived.

He jumped into his plain old 1950 Dodge that, as was required by the Old Order Mennonite Order his family belonged to, was without any chrome or shiny hubcaps. Adam wished that he could have a car like the ones that he saw when he drove into town—the ones with shiny chrome, shiny hubcaps, cars that were newer and had a look of success when driven down the street. But he was satisfied that he at least owned a car that was dependable. He liked his old car and would be sad to give it up if he ever traded it in for a newer one.

Adam drove the six miles down the sand and gravel road toward the Goering farm. When he reached their lengthy driveway, he pulled in toward their house, the back of which faced the driveway. So, what was visible consisted of the back porch and the door that led into the kitchen.

Something didn't look right as he pulled up to the back of the Goering house. A car was parked there that didn't appear to be one that would belong to a member of their Mennonite Order. It was sleek shiny red car with mirror-like chrome bumpers, chrome strips on the sides, and shiny hubcaps that appeared to be made of spoked chrome that glistened in the last rays of the sun as it was descending onto the horizon. It was definitely not one that he would expect to be parked at the Goering house, unless it was a salesman or someone like that.

Still looking admiringly at the beautiful car, Adam exited his old car. He walked briskly and happily to the back door of the Goering house and opened the screen door onto the back porch. He walked onto the porch and knocked loudly enough on the door that led to the kitchen so that it could be heard inside the kitchen and living room. He expected Sarah to come to the door since their evening together was to begin at 7:00 pm, and it was exactly that time when he arrived. Instead, Sarah's mother met him at the door, and opened it slightly to acknowledge Adam's arrival. That was all. He thought it strange that she didn't appear to be inviting him into their home. She stood in the partially opened door with a rather strained look on her face.

"Hello Adam," she said. Even her voice sounded strange, and she was looking from side to side and not at Adam. She began hesitantly, "Sarah…uh…has company at this moment, and she isn't able to come to the door. Would you like to return later? Or…perhaps…come back tomorrow?"

Adam was very much taken back by Sarah's mother's strange actions and her words, "But, Sarah and I had plans for this evening. I was to meet to here at 7:00 pm. Is something wrong?" He wanted to know what was going on. Why was she not available to see him?

Sarah's mother was obviously searching for words of explanation. "She…uh…has a visitor who she was not expecting. I'm not sure how long this visitor will be here. Sarah's father is also involved in their…uh…conversation."

"But," Adam continued, "we had plans for this evening. Can't she explain that to her visitor, and perhaps she or he could return at another time." Adam was becoming concerned that something was definitely not as it should be with Sarah. Something was very wrong.

"I don't think that is possible at this time, Adam," Sarah's mother was obviously distraught—something was wrong in the Goering house that she did not want to divulge to Adam. "I am sure that Sarah will explain the situation when she sees you next. That is all that I can say now, Adam. I'm sorry." Then she closed the door to the kitchen.

Adam stood looking at the closed door for a few moments. He didn't know what to say. He desperately wanted to know what was going on inside of the Goering house. He and Sarah had plans for this evening, and he didn't feel that she would cancel them like this without letting him know earlier. What had happened? What was going on inside of the Goering house that made her mother deny him entrance? Why was her father involved?

As he stood at the door, he had heard loud voices, and some voices that sounded rather strained and even louder—shouting, in fact. He could hear Sarah's father's voice along with those of Sarah. He could still hear loud voices through the closed door although he was not able to understand the words that were being said. He desperately wished that he could. Was Richie there? What was happening?

Adam felt like he did when Sarah had suddenly left with Richie a few years earlier—as though someone had hit him in the stomach. He felt ill. He didn't know what to do! He wanted to talk to Sarah to find out what was wrong. He was angry—he was hurt—he desperately wanted to see Sarah to find out what was happening.

But what could he do? At this point, all he could do was leave and drive back home. He walked back to his car, and as he did so, he noticed once again the shiny sleek car that was sitting in the driveway. Was it Richie? Could it be that he has returned for Sarah? Was that it? Was that why he was not allowed inside the Goering house, why Sarah couldn't see him? And why was her father involved in the loud confrontation that was apparently going on in the Goering house? It must be something very serious.

Adam drove slowly back home. Despondent and angry, he entered his family's house and started to walk to the stairway that led to his bedroom. When his mother and father saw him, they asked why he was not with Sarah. Adam was in such a high state of emotion that when he looked at them, tears were beginning to well up in his eyes. He turned, not wanting his parents to see the tears that were starting to run down his cheeks. He grabbed the handkerchief that he kept in his pocket, blew his nose and wiped his face so that it would look like nothing was bothering him.

"I don't know," he finally replied softly, trying to regain his composure. "Something is going on in the Goering house, and no one would tell me anything while I stood at the back door. Sarah couldn't come to the door, and her mother wouldn't let me into the house. Her father was somehow involved, but I don't know how or why. I could hear his loud voice that sounded angry. I could hear several loud voices in their house that sounded very angry!"

"There was a very sleek and shiny car sitting in their driveway, and I have a suspicion that it might belong to Richie Johnson, the one Sarah ran away with a couple of years ago. But I don't know. All I know is that something is wrong, but I don't know what it is."

At those words, Adam turned and climbed the stairs to his bedroom while his parents remained in the kitchen, not knowing what to say. Once again Adam felt as though he had been hit in the stomach with a large fist. He felt ill.

He fell onto his bed. He was still fully clothed but didn't feel like getting ready for bed just yet. The evening that he had looked forward to all week was ruined by someone, but he wasn't sure who it was. He suspected that it was Richie Johnson who had returned to reunite with Sarah. But, why? He had deserted her—abandoned her, and their community had declared him and their marriage dead after a year when he did not return. Sarah was, according to the doctrine of their Old Order Mennonite Order, no longer married to Richie, plus she had their marriage annulled by a judge in a court of law in the town where he had left her.

She and Adam had been seeing each other and were beginning to rekindle their relationship for which he had patiently waited nearly three years. He desperately wanted to talk to Sarah to find out what had happened, and why he could not see her that evening. Why had her mother acted so strangely? Why was he not allowed to enter their house? Why was he obviously not welcome? Why was her father involved? Why the loud voices that were coming from their house? Why had Sarah's mother held the screen door that led into their kitchen only partially open while she talked to Adam, as though she was afraid that he might attempt to enter their house? Something that he was not to see or hear was obviously going on inside their house, and he was not allowed to determine what it was.

It was time for Adam to turn in for the night. It was now 10:00 pm, an hour he would have been spending with Sarah. Not being with her hurt badly, so much so that his body ached. But what could he do? What should he do? He felt helpless at this point. Why didn't Sarah call him to tell him what had happened, to explain why she was unable to be with him that evening? She had access to a telephone. Or was the someone who was there at the Goering house keeping her attention to the degree that she could not or did not want to call him to explain. He could call her. But, on second thought if she did not or could not come to the phone, it would only make matters worse. So, he dismissed that possibility.

Not really wanting to, but needing to brush his teeth, he put on his pajamas and crawled into bed. The extreme anxiety that he had felt over the past several hours had exhausted him. He felt weak and ill. His head hurt and his well-toned muscles felt as though he had been lifting heavy weights all evening. They had been held in rigid state of tension for so long that they, too, were exhausted.

Maybe Sarah will call tomorrow to explain, Adam thought as he was drifting off to sleep. He needed an explanation—he deserved an explanation. It was not like Sarah to 'brush him off' when they had made plans for the evening. Adam wanted to know what was happening. He wanted to know the reason why he was not allowed to enter their house when he drove over to meet Sarah for their evening together. His mind was a jumble—everything he had waited for, hoped for, needed, suddenly seemed to be drifting away!

Chapter 28

Morning came after a fitful night of partial wakefulness. He had drifted off to sleep only to awaken worrying about Sarah, wondering, wishing that he could talk with her, then drifting off to sleep again only to awaken once more. He was tired, he was angry, he was worried, he was disappointed, he was…in a state of confusion. He only wanted to talk with Sarah to find out what had happened the night before.

Today was Sunday, and Sunday meant church. Would Sarah be there? Would he be allowed to see her? Would he be allowed to talk to her? Adam began putting on his work clothes since he had chores to complete before he would be able to get dressed for church. As he dressed, he continued to wonder why Sarah didn't call to explain about the previous evening? Why? Something must be terribly wrong.

Just then he heard the phone ring downstairs in the kitchen. He then heard his mother answer and after a moment she told the caller that she would call him to the phone. Adam's heart jumped, a lump grew in his throat. He was only partially dressed, but enough so that he was decent when he ran down the stairs almost tripping as he cleared the stairs two at a time. He was desperately hoping that it was Sarah who was calling him. His mother was just getting set to call him to the phone when he was already standing next to her ready to take the receiver. She quietly said, "It's Sarah."

Adam, his voice quivering slightly uttered, "Hello?"

"Adam, it's Sarah. Oh Adam, I owe you a huge apology. I didn't know what to do. I need to talk with you…will you be a church this morning?"

"Yes—I'll be there," he replied. "I can see you there, but can I see you after church like this afternoon? Church really isn't a good place to talk. I want to see you."

There was a pause on Sarah's end, and finally she replied, "We'll see after I talk with you…I'll see you at church."

That was all. Sarah said goodbye and hung up the receiver on her end. Adam was left with a huge void—there was no closure. She didn't say anything about the evening before, she didn't say that she was sorry that she canceled the evening they were supposed to be together, she didn't say anything really that made any sense except that she owes him an apology. Something was wrong!

At least he was going to be able to see Sarah. That was a relief! She was not avoiding him for some reason that he wasn't aware of. Maybe there will be some closure after they talk.

Adam finished putting on his work clothes and went outside to complete the morning chores that he was responsible for. He had completed feeding calves their fortified breakfast, putting down bales of alfalfa hay for the dairy cows and his beef cattle and taking them out to the feed troughs, and then making sure that all had water. He had completed those morning chores so many times during his young life that it had become nearly automatic. After he completed those responsibilities, he looked back to make sure that all was completed satisfactorily. He said 'Good morning' to his father who was finishing milking the dairy cows, and began his walk back to their house for breakfast.

He wasn't necessarily as hungry as he usually was in the morning. He was so concerned about what Sarah might say to him that his only thought was to get to church, sit through the service and then hopefully meet with Sarah somewhere where they could talk without being overheard by others.

After his breakfast, Adam climbed the stairs to his room to change from his work clothes into clothes that were appropriate to be worn to church. Those included a white shirt without a collar, homemade slacks that were held up by wide suspenders, stockings that matched his slacks at least to some degree, and his best shoes. His flat brimmed brown felt hat that he wore was the standard for Old Order Mennonite. When he was dressed and ready for church, he went to the corral to find Ginger as he did every Sunday morning in order to prepare the horse and buggy for the ride to church. When he had Ginger hitched to the buggy, he climbed in and drove close to the house, tied Ginger securely to the fence, and went into the kitchen to tell his mother and father that everything was ready.

The ride to church via horse and buggy was a tradition with the Yoder family. Quite a few other members of their church did the same, feeling that it was keeping something of their Old Order Mennonite traditions alive. Also, it was fun and relaxing to drive a horse and buggy slowly along their country roads to church. It gave a person time to think, relax and prepare for worship. Adam, however, was wishing that they could move along faster to arrive at church sooner so that he could be assured that Sarah was keeping her promise that she would be attending that day.

They finally arrived at the Wheatland Old Order Mennonite Church, pulled into the parking area where horses and buggies were kept during the church service. After his parents left the buggy to walk into the church, Adam drove Ginger over to the open water tank that was in the middle of the parking area so she could have a drink of water. After Ginger was parked along the side of the parking area with the other horses and buggies, Adam placed a feed bag filled with plenty of corn on Ginger so she would have something to eat while she was waiting for the return of the family for the drive home after the church service was over for the day.

As soon as he parked their 'Sunday go-to-church buggy', Adam walked swiftly toward the church entrance so that he could see if Sarah had arrived. When he arrived at the front door of the church and looked inside, he was relieved to see Sarah sitting with her parents in about the middle of the sanctuary. When Adam's parents caught up with him at the front door, they walked in together and found seats near the back of the sanctuary at the end of a pew. Adam was happy at that seating position so that when the last 'amen' was said at the conclusion of the church service, he could exit the pew in a hurry to catch Sarah so that they could go somewhere and talk.

It seemed as though the church service would never end. The preacher, Reverend Jacob Koehn was going on and on about the sins of the world, and how we were not to succumb to temptations of 'the world' (although Adam happened to know quite a few of their community who fermented beer in their own cellars and drank it cold out in the fields during the hot days of summer, and some even made their own wine!). Finally, Reverend Koehn stopped preaching and the collection plates were passed through the congregation. Nearly everyone put something in the plates either in an envelope or cash and the ushers ceremoniously took the nearly full copper plates down to the alter at the front of the sanctuary. Then all five verses of the final hymn were sung, the benediction was slowly repeated by the preacher, and the service was finally over.

As soon as the final words of the benediction were said, Adam leaned to the left to tell his mother and father that he was going to catch Sarah and talk for a little bit before they headed toward home. They indicated approval and Adam bolted from the pew and headed to the center of the sanctuary to wait for Sarah who was just leaving her family's pew and entering the center aisle.

Adam waited patiently for a few moments as Sarah and her family talked briefly with other members of their church as they walked slowly up the isle toward the back of the sanctuary. Adam was now waiting by the primary exit as Sarah and her family approached. He walked toward her and expected her to acknowledge his presence so they could leave the sanctuary and walk outside where they could talk. Instead, Sarah looked down, not really acknowledging the presence of Adam, and was apparently intending to walk on by with her family.

Adam touched Sarah's arm and was expecting her to see him and move toward him so that they could move away from family and friends and talk for a few moments. Rather, she seemed to try to move away from Adam. Not wanting to seem too aggressive, but still desiring to talk with her alone, he took her arm and moved her at least somewhat forcefully away from her family and over by the side of the church in a shady spot.

"Sarah," Adam said quickly, "don't you want to talk with me? You said on the phone that we could talk." He quickly continued, "I just want to know why you apparently couldn't be with me last night? Why your mother would not allow me to enter your house? Why the fancy car was parked in your driveway? Why your mother wouldn't tell me why you couldn't be with me on our date? We had a date to be together last night that you seemed happy about, but suddenly you were not available to be with me. Why? I felt hurt—I was very sad, and it was difficult for me to understand what was happening. Can you explain? Please explain so I will understand."

Sarah was quiet for a moment, looking down at the sparsely growing grass that was growing on the lawn of the church. Finally she began slowly speaking in an almost inaudible manner. "Richie was there at our home. He drove in at about 5:00 pm and wanted to see me. He had driven from visiting his mother and father who are still living north of here in the Lutheran community. I was so surprised to see him. It has been over two years since I last saw him when he left me. I didn't think that I would ever see him again. But there he was as big as life, and with another beautiful shiny car."

"What did he want?" Adam asked. "Why after all this time would he come to see you? Why couldn't you tell him that you had plans for the evening and couldn't see him? Why wasn't I allowed to see you?"

Sarah replied, "I didn't know what to do. He simply knocked on our door and mother let him in. *Why* she allowed him into our house, I cannot imagine. He was suddenly just there in our house. What was I to do, Adam?"

"You could have told him to leave! He left you; he is considered dead by our church. He does not exist in accordance with the beliefs of our Mennonite doctrine. He is no longer a part of your life. Why would you permit him to be with you or you with him?" Adam said in a louder whispered voice than he probably should have since there were so many of the church members standing nearby.

"Please talk in a softer voice, Adam," Sarah replied. "Others will hear you."

"I really do not care." Adam said in a tense near-breathy whisper. "I don't care! Richie left you—he has been pronounced dead by our church. He hurt you, Sarah. You are no longer married, and I want you to be with me. I love you, Sarah!" Adam said in voice so loud that the church members standing nearby turned to see who was talking. Smiling, they nodded and acknowledged that two young people were obviously acknowledging their commitment to each other.

"Shhhhhh," Sarah had placed her index finger against her lips to quiet Adam. "You are embarrassing me. We need to go someplace else where we can talk and not be heard," she said in a rather forceful manner.

"I'm sorry," Adam replied. "I guess that I cannot understand why he came to see you, and why you allowed him to take away our evening together. That's what I would like to know."

"If you'll let me, I'll explain," Sarah said in reply. "Again, we need to go someplace where people won't be able to hear our conversation. Can we go someplace this evening—even it's just in your car? We could go to the M & J Drive-In and have the root beer you told me about. There we could talk and people wouldn't be standing near us to listen."

Adam thought for a moment and then said, "OK. As long as Richie won't be at your house to interfere with our time together."

"Adam, that really hurt!" Sarah replied quickly. "Why would you say such a thing. I didn't invite Richie to our home, I hope you understand. He just arrived and I didn't know what to do. Now, you have *me* talking too loudly. That's all that I will say for now. What time will you come by to pick me up?"

"How about after supper—about 7:00 pm?"

"Sounds fine," Sarah said in reply. "I'll see you then." She then turned and walked toward her family and confirmed that she was riding home with them.

Adam walked slowly toward the parking lot where their horse Ginger stood patiently, still attached to their buggy. Adam removed the feed bag and led her to the watering tank so she could have another drink of water. His parents saw him at the buggy, and so ceased their conversation with their church friends and walked to the parking lot and climbed in. Adam took the reins, snapped them on Ginger's rump, gave two clicks with his tongue and they were off and out of the parking lot onto the road toward home.

Adam was quiet during their ride home, still thinking about Sarah, and wishing that he knew what she was going to say when they were together that evening. At least he knew that they would be together and could talk. That was a relief to him. Then he would know where he stood in the eyes of Sarah. He hoped and prayed that Richie wouldn't be there.

After they arrived at their home, and as soon as the Sunday noon meal was served and the Yoder family had finished eating, Adam left the dinner table and walked outside. He wanted to be alone. He wanted some time to think. That evening, he and Sarah would be together, or at least he hoped all would go according to plan and they would be together to talk. What would occur during their evening together? Well—he simply needed some time alone and some time to think and plan what he might hear and say in return.

In order to be absolutely alone, Adam had a special place where he could think, meditate, problem-solve, and sing songs that he made up where no one heard him. In order to be in his special place, he had to walk about one-half of a mile diagonally across one of their wheat fields to a place where a house and outbuildings of an old farmstead once stood. The house, barn and outbuildings had been demolished long ago, and all that remained were three tall shade trees and a mound of dirt that covered what used to be the family's cellar that was located next to the house. The old stone stairway to the cellar was still there but was mostly filled with dirt. For whatever reason, he had never taken the time to work his way down into that old stairway primarily because he didn't care for spiders and didn't want to encounter any. But his special place was under those three trees in the shade where he would sit quietly.

In that remote place, out there in that wheat field under the trees he was away from everything and everybody. No one could see him because of the undergrowth. The only sound came from the wind and the rustling of the leaves of those three old elm trees. The leaves produced a wonderfully lonely rustling sound. Nothing else could be heard.

That was his special place, his sanctuary away from the rest of the world where he could think, pray, problem-solve, meditate, and grow into manhood away from the distractions of a busy world.

Adam felt that everyone needed their own special place. It may not be in the corner of a wheat field, but it can be a corner of a person's home where there is a picture or a window view that is calming—one they could look at and remember, dream a little, clear their mind and regenerate. Sometimes just a few moments of silence and reflection can do wonders—bringing peace of mind and a few moments of calm to an otherwise hectic day. Adam felt that everyone should have their own quiet special place.

This afternoon, however, his thoughts were with Sarah. What had happened to what he felt was the rebirth of their relationship—the relationship that he felt was becoming closer since her return—the potential for their future? His dream was for her to be his wife and the mother of their children. That had been his dream for longer than he could remember. She had left, literally run away, but then had returned. He had hoped that her return would mean the beginning of the continuance of their relationship, or at least what he had hoped was their relationship and the beginning of a romance that could lead to their love for each other, and beyond.

Those were his thoughts on that quiet afternoon in his 'thinking place', his quiet place where he was alone with his thoughts and dreams of Sarah.

Chapter 29

Since it was Sunday afternoon and on Sundays there was no field work, Adam felt a welcome relief. After sitting for some time in the shade of the old elm trees in what used to be the front yard of that old farmhouse, he realized by the position of the sun that it must be getting late in the afternoon. He glanced at this watch, saw that it was 4:00 pm, and realized that it was much later than he had intended to remain there. He still had chores to complete before supper, and he wanted to clean up—at least shave, brush his teeth and change into better cleaner clothes before leaving to be with Sarah.

So, he began walking back across the field toward their house. The one half mile across the field seemed longer when returning than when going to his quiet place. He walked as fast as he could in the soft earth—his boots sinking a little with every step. His legs became very tired, but he kept going. He had to get his chores done as quickly as possible.

When he arrived back at the farm stead, he walked quickly to the house to have a drink of water since he had forgotten to bring his water bottle with him. Then he returned to the barn to begin the chores he was responsible for. By 5:30 pm, he had completed feeding the calves, putting hay bales onto the bed of the old pickup trucks that he drove around to the back of the main barn where he broke the bales into sheaves and put them in the long feed bunks for the dairy cows and his beef cattle to eat. He then made sure that all animals had plenty of water, and then completed the other chores for which he was responsible.

When those were finished, Adam walked back to the house and into the bathroom that was off the kitchen. He was still sweating from the long walk back to their farmstead and the chores he was to complete, so he took a quick shower, ran a razor across his face to remove any extra rough whiskers and combed his hair. Adam then went upstairs to the second floor of their house to change his clothes and prepare to drive over to the Goering farm after supper to meet Sarah for their evening together.

What his mother was cooking smelled good—baked pork chops, fried potatoes with spicy brown gravy, green beans, yeast rolls with plenty of homemade butter, and apple pie for dessert. That is what the Yoder family called a good farm-style Sunday supper. Although he should have been hungry, his appetite had diminished somewhat as result of his concerns about his upcoming evening with Sarah. Those thoughts and fears dominated his usual ample appetite.

The meal that his mother had prepared was sitting before him, and it looked wonderful. But he simply didn't feel hungry at the moment. Maybe if the evening with Sarah went well, he would be able to snack when he returned later. His mother and father were having difficulty understanding the change in their son's appetite until Adam admitted that he was worried about the evening with Sarah, and simply did not feel like eating right then. His mother smiled in an understanding way and said that she would keep a plate of food for him in the refrigerator if he wanted to re-heat it and eat later. Adam nodded and said that that sounded good, and that he appreciated it.

Adam then went upstairs to look in the mirror on the dresser to make sure that his hair was well combed, and he added just an extra touch of aftershave to his face. He then sat on the edge of his large soft bed. He was more tired than he expected to be. Perhaps it was the long walk back from his quiet place. The walk was a tiring one, but it shouldn't have made him this tired. And he knew that it wasn't from completing the evening chores for which he was responsible. He did these every morning and evening and was used to doing them well. But perhaps it was from his worrying and concerns about his evening with Sarah—what she might say and where their relationship might be headed.

In any event, he wanted to look his best, so he took one final look in the bedroom mirror and decided that he was ready to see Sarah. He didn't want to appear to be worried and tired from wondering and worrying about Sarah. He wanted to look fresh and as handsome as he possibly could. In other words, he wanted to impress Sarah in such a way that she would forget about Richie.

It was now 6:45 pm and time for him to jump in his car and drive over to the Goering farm to meet Sarah.

Adam felt rather apprehensive as he drove over to the Goering's. He was afraid that when he drove into their driveway, Richie's car would be sitting in front of their house. He felt the retching in his stomach that he would feel if he was there…unannounced, brazen, self-assured, walking into the Goering's house as though he belonged there. Did he not know that Sarah had their marriage annulled nearly a year ago? And that in the eyes and doctrine of their conservative Mennonite Order Richie was considered dead, so Sarah was not bound to 'Till death do you part'? Did he not know that? Had Sarah, her father or mother not told him? Why was he even allowed into their house last Saturday evening?

He pulled into the driveway of the Goering's farm and to his relief Richie's car wasn't there. He walked to the back door of their farmhouse, walked across the porch and knocked on the door. Sarah greeted him and invited him inside. As soon as he walked in, she called to tell her mother that Adam was there and they would be leaving for a while to get a root beer at the L & M Root Beer Drive-In.

Her mother called back with a happy tone in her voice, "Have a good time!"

Sarah and Adam walked to his car and Adam opened the passenger side door for Sarah. She jumped in and was smiling when Adam entered the driver's side.

They drove into Wheatland, Kansas, with the L & M Root Beer drive-in as their destination. Both were rather silent during that short drive, but Jacob mentioned the barbeque hamburgers that he was anxious to try and mentioned that the root beer was supposed to be excellent. He was trying to fill the void of silence that was coming from Sarah's side of the front seat.

When they arrived at the drive-in, Jacob found a rather out of the way spot where they could park and order their snacks, a spot that was not in front of the bright lights that filled the area where the attendants came and went with orders that were taken to the cars that were parked around the drive-in.

As it had been at the truck stop where they had spent their evening of talking the week before, silence filled Jacob's car as they ordered their hamburger and root beer and then waited for their orders to be delivered. Jacob was about to use the same amusing start of conversation that Sarah had used at the truck stop, "I am sure you are wondering why I called this meeting—"

But, before he could use that phrase, Sarah broke the silence by talking in a rapid sequence of words that sounded as though they had been rehearsed, "Jacob, I am so sorry that our date was interrupted last evening. I was looking forward to being with you, but then Richie entered our house with my mother's consent and walked right into our living room. I am not sure why my mother allowed him to enter our house, but in a way I am pleased that she did. The reason I am pleased is that my family and I were able to clarify some things with him."

"What I mean by 'clarify' is I was hoping that he would be made completely aware that he was to leave and never return. You might have had heard some of our loud voices as you were standing by the back door. I'm pretty sure that you would have since we were speaking rather loudly and forcefully to Richie."

Jacob acknowledged what Sarah said, "Yes, I did hear voices coming from what I thought might be the living room, one being your father. I could tell by his voice. However, I couldn't understand what was being said."

Otherwise, Jacob sat quietly while Sarah spoke, not knowing quite what else to say at that time.

Sarah continued: "I don't know why Richie decided to drive over to our house. He wanted to see if I would like to go for a ride in his new car. I didn't see it, but I am supposing that it was a shiny and sporty model. I didn't want to see it. One of his shiny new cars is partially what enticed me to run away with him in the first place. I don't want to see his cars anymore!"

Sarah continued in a more intense manner, "In the first place, I didn't want to see him again. But he walked into our living room, sat down as though he owned our house and began to talk about his plans, his great future, and had the gall to ask why I didn't wait for him in the apartment where I lived alone for a year."

"My father and I interrupted him while he was carrying on his self-aggrandized conversation and asked him in a rather forceful way, 'Why did you come here, Richie? What was your reason for coming into our house?'"

Richie looked rather taken aback, opened his mouth and began to say that he came to take his wife back with him. He seemed to think that Sarah had run away from him and wanted her back.

Sarah replied in her strongest voice, "Richie, after you left me, I waited for you for an entire year to return to the awful place where I was living. During that time, I realized what a terrible mistake I had made when I literally ran away with you to discover what I thought would be a new adventure in my life. I realized during that year that marrying you was an awful mistake—a mistake that may have ruined my life and ruined everything that I loved back home. So, I went to a court of law and spoke to a judge who happily agreed with me that I had made a terrible mistake in marrying a man who was not of my Mennonite Order, and who obviously did not love me. He agreed to rule legally that our marriage was irreversibly broken and agreed that an annulment was in order. Our marriage was annulled by that judge in a court of law. So, our marriage is dead! It no longer exists!"

"Further, in accordance with our Old Order Mennonite doctrine, our marriage is dead, and so are *you*, Richie." "You are *dead* in the eyes of our family, my Mennonite Order, and our community. I have been welcomed back to my family, my church, and the young man who loves me, and so my life has returned to what it was before I recklessly abandoned what I loved and ran away with *you*. I am back home where I will remain, and I never want to see you again, Richie Johnson!"

Sarah concluded, "Then my father entered the conversation at that point and told Richie in a loud voice to leave and *never* return to our farm. He said it in a loud, forceful manner that I had never heard him use before. I am sure that is what you might have heard when you were at the back door of our house. Even though according to our beliefs and our church doctrine, we as Old Order Mennonites are peaceful and non-combatant. However, my father said rather forcefully that if Richie returns to our farm and tries to contact me, he would, if necessary be willing to call the sheriff and have him removed for trespassing."

"Wow!" Adam responded. "I had no idea that was the conversation that was taking place when I arrived last evening to pick you up for our date. I am so sorry that you had to go through all that turmoil when you weren't expecting it."

Sarah replied, "Well…I wanted you to know what had happened last evening that ruined our time together. Again, I had no idea that Richie was going to come to our house and try to entice me to go with him in his new car. I am so pleased that my father was there with me to forcefully tell Richie that he was not to see me again. It was such a relief that he was there. Richie finally left and drove away. I am thinking that I won't see him again. At least I *HOPE* with all my heart that I won't see him again."

For the remainder of their time together, Sarah and Jacob received their special hamburgers and root beers and enjoyed being together. Sarah told Jacob that it was so very nice to be with him, and that she feels at peace when they are together. Feeling *at peace* was what she needed and one of many reasons why she loved being with him. She looked intently at Jacob and said quietly that this is where she felt that she belonged…that is, she belonged to be with him.

Jacob replied, "I love you, Sarah." And she leaned over and gave him a hamburger-flavored kiss on his cheek.

After they completed eating their barbeque hamburger and drinking their root beer, they felt that it was time to complete their time together. So, Jacob drove Sarah back to the Goering farm. After a hug and a soulful kiss, it was time to say 'Goodnight'.

Chapter 30

Just as they were leaving Adam's car and beginning their walk toward the Goering's house to say goodnight, a glistening red and cream two-door convertible pulled up behind Adam's plain 1950 Dodge. It came to a sudden sliding stop that brought with it a cloud of dust that showered Adam and Sarah. Who else, but Ritchie Johnson was sitting behind the wheel. He jumped out of the car and walked swiftly toward Adam and Sarah, appearing confident in his approach, purposely avoiding Adam as though he hadn't noticed that he was there.

"Hey Sarah, goin' somewhere?" he said with assurance, indicating in the sound of his voice that he had some authority in the matter. "I just ran over to see if we could go for a ride—maybe go into town for a while." He ignored the fact that Adam was standing next to Sarah, as though he didn't really exist, or at least didn't care that he existed. His goal was obviously to talk Sarah into leaving with him.

Sarah was startled, and for a moment didn't know what to say. How *dare* Richie drive over and expect her to leave Adam and go someplace with him. How could he be so brazen, with so much assumed authority over her? How arrogant of him! He *knew* he wasn't supposed to be at the Goering house. Sarah's father had told him the evening before that he would be willing to call the sheriff to take him away if he came to their farm again. Richie obviously felt that the threat was an empty one.

Sarah, her face turning red walked up to Richie and said in her loudest voice, "I want to remind you, Richie, that yesterday evening you were told to NEVER come to this house again. You were told in no uncertain terms that you were supposed to stay away. Did you not understand what you were told by me and my father?"

In an even louder voice and with greater speed, Sarah continued, "You were told *directly* that you were to leave and NOT return. How *unthinking* of you that you could feel that you could drive over to our house knowing full well that you are not to be here, and expect me to drive away with you?"

That was what nearly three years earlier caused Sarah to leave her family, her church and Adam. It was Richie's self-assurance that she would do whatever he wanted her to do. He seemed to have some sort of hypnotic power that drew people to do exactly what he wanted.

But, no more! She would *NOT* do what he wanted her to do. Did he want Sarah to return to the nightmare that she had experienced for the past two years? Was that his intent—his desire?

Sarah walked slowly toward Richie. Her face was rigid, her teeth were clinched, her fists were held tightly at her side. She walked to within 12 inches of Richie's face, looked at him squarely and then spit on him. She spit in his face, and through tightly clenched teeth said with as much feeling as she could muster, she screamed as loudly as she could, "I want you *off* this property now. If you *ever* return, my father will greet you. He is not a violent man, but when he becomes riled, and when he is finished with you, you will wish that you had never been born, Richie Johnson. Although we are non-combative in our Mennonite Order, as my father told you we can still call the sheriff and have you arrested for trespassing."

"Now," she hissed with feeling into his face, "get in that shiny car of yours, drive away and *never* return! You made my life *hell* when we were married. This past year after you had deserted me I had our marriage annulled, and it is legal and binding. Our Mennonite doctrine has proclaimed you to be *dead*, Richie Johnson. Our marriage is *dead,* and I hope that in the eyes of God I am not condemned because I wish *you were dead*, Richie. Now LEAVE! I *never* want to see you again. *Leave*!" she screamed. Sarah's body was shaking as she drew back from his face and walked away toward Adam's car.

Adam was standing next to the open door on the driver's side of his car. He stood still, not knowing what to do or say. But then mustering the courage that he wasn't sure he had or had ever experienced, he walked slowly over to Richie who was still standing affixed by his shiny new car. Richie's eyes were wide, and his mouth stood open while Sarah's spit was running down his chin, he not knowing what to say.

Adam stood in front of Richie as close as he could and looked sternly into his eyes. After a moment of drama filled silence, he said with a guttural growl, "You are to be leaving, Richie—*now*! It is time. As Sarah said, in the eyes of our Mennonite Order, her father and mother, and all others, and in the eyes of God, as her husband you are considered *dead*. And your marriage has been legally annulled by a judge in the Courts of Law. So, it is dead. It is time for you to go away and leave Sarah alone. If you don't, Sarah's father and I will both confront you in a way you will *always* regret." Adam turned and walked toward Sarah. He took her hand, and they walked together into her family's house.

Richie stood by his new car. He looked strangely pale and was visibly shaken. He grasped his handkerchief and wiped the spittle from his face that Sarah had in her fury placed there. His mouth stood open, eyes open wide, shoulders slumped. He turned slowly and opened the door to his car. He then sat behind the steering wheel still staring blankly, transfixed as if on something, but on nothing.

This had never happened to him before. He always achieved what he desired. He never failed to conquer the female he desired. He never expected what had happened to him now. He had failed in his conquest of a woman!

Richie placed his hand on the ignition key to his shiny new car, the type of car he used in order to get what he wanted from women. It had worked on Sarah before, but she had changed. Something had changed her…what or who had changed her? What had happened to her? He had relied on his charm, and as always, a flashy new car was used to attract women to him. They seemed to allow themselves to be conquered by him. And it always worked. Their souls were so easily conquered.

Oh well, there were other fish, or women, in the sea. He would find another soul to conquer…So, with his usual look of arrogance he turned the key to the ignition, the engine came alive with a roar, his foot stomped on the gas, the rear wheels spun raising dust and rocks as he wheeled the car around and sped out of the driveway and down the main road out of Sarah's life.

Sarah and Adam were standing by the window in the Goering's house that looked out over the back yard onto the driveway. They saw Richie standing by his car looking perplexed, staring into nothing. Then they saw him get into his car, heard him start the engine and spin the rear tires raising dust and gravel into the air as he drove rapidly onto the main road heading south. Where he was going they did not know, nor did they care. They were both still shaking a little, their adrenaline still working, and Adam still had hold of Sarah's hand. He hadn't let go until he knew they were safe in her house.

A few moments later, when their emotional state had settled a little, Adam looked at Sarah, looked deep into her eyes and said with deep emotion, "You were wonderful out there, Sarah. You told Richie exactly how you felt—you drew down deep into yourself and *really* told him, I think, everything you have been holding back over the past several years. It all came out perfectly with all of the anger and hurt and regret you seem to have felt for quite a while. I was very proud of you, Sarah! I wanted to give you a great big hug of congratulations."

"And you too, Adam," Sarah replied. "I was proud of you when you told Richie what would happen to him if he bothered me again. I was pleased with the emotion you seemed to release when you told him. I think that he truly believed what you said. He seemed shocked and in disbelief. He didn't know what to think. He felt that he could conquer me, hypnotize me, take me away again. But I think that you and I convinced him it wasn't going to work. I don't think he will return. But, if he should, he will receive just what you and I let him know would happen to him.”

Then, Sarah looked deeply into Adam's eyes and held them there for what seemed a long time. But at the moment, time didn't seem very important. As their eyes lingered upon each other, Sarah broke the silence and quietly said, “Adam…we have known each other for many years now. You have silently waited for me to grow up, to get over my rebellion against my family, my Mennonite upbringing, my desire to ‘see the world’.”

“But you have waited for me out of your love and devotion to me, and your faith, your hope that I would someday return to be with you. Out of all your patience, you somehow knew that we would at some time be together again. And I want you to know that out of all your patience and devotion to me, I have grown to realize that I love you.”

“Oh…I love you, dear Adam, with all my heart, I love you! I want to be with you. I don't want to be without you. And, if you will have me, I want to be yours to have and to hold for always!” Her tears swelled and ran down her now rose-colored cheeks. And those same tears fell from Adam's eyes as they were now cradled in each other's arms.

The End